NANCY BETH TRAYES

MYSTERY MOUNTAIN

By the author of
THE MYSTERY OF THE MC GILLEY MANSION

YOUNG AMERICA BOOK CLUB · EDUCATION CENTER · COLUMBUS, OHIO 43216

MYSTERY
MOUNTAIN

Florence Laughlin

ILLUSTRATED BY *Barbara Werner*

Macrae Smith Company / PHILADELPHIA

FOR MY FAVORITE TWINS,
Douglas and Bentham McKay

Contents

MYSTERY MOUNTAIN

1
Danny Meets His Double

"Come along, slowpoke."

Dan Glover twisted in his saddle, calling urgently to his sister Karen, who had been mosying along behind him on her small pinto mare.

"If we don't hurry back to the ranch we'll get soaked," Dan shouted. "It'll be raining cats and polliwogs soon."

"I don't care if it does."

Twelve-year-old Karen gave her horse a clip with her heel and cantered up alongside her older brother. The wind blew the dark hair back from her face, and her eyes were suddenly aglow with excitement. "I love thunderstorms!" she declared.

The storm had risen with little warning, as is often the case on the deserts of Arizona in summertime. An hour before, when the two young people rode from the ranch to fetch the mail from the box near the highway, the sky had been clear and blue. Now it was dark and threatening.

Lightning flashed in the hills and thunder growled among the clouds.

Dan took a deep gulp of the ozone-rich air, sharing his sister's joy in the storm, but at the same time he made Chili, his horse, move on a bit faster. He knew that Great-aunt Charlotte would be watching for them at the ranch, and that she would be anxious if they were late.

"You know how superstitious Aunt Chat is about riding in bad weather," he called loudly to Karen.

"That's because there was such a terrible storm the night her father was lost on the mountain," the girl shouted back. "But that was years and years ago. Aunt Chat was just a little girl. I don't believe she really remembers the storm. She has heard people talk about that night so often that she just thinks she remembers——"

"She was five," Dan retorted. "Sometimes very old people recall things from their childhood better than they do the events of yesterday. Besides"—he looked up at the rugged peaks that towered behind the rangeland of his great-aunt's ranch—"how could anybody ever forget a storm on old Mystery? Look at it now!"

Almost without thought both young riders relaxed reins. They stared spellbound at the spectacle of nature before them.

Mystery Mountain was impressive enough in bright sunlight, but now, with its great crags rising like fangs into the ink-blue clouds, with giant pitchforks of lightning stabbing its canyons, it appeared more awesome than ever. It was beautiful, dangerous, challenging, and all the more fascinating to Karen and Dan because somewhere in that vast wasteland lay the answer to the mystery of the strange disappearance of their great-grandfather, over seventy years before.

It had been a summer day then, too, when the young English rancher, Daniel Glover the First, rode up into those hills to visit the rich gold mine he had uncovered there. He had left his wife and two children in the adobe ranch house below, promising to return within a few days.

The first night, his campfire on Signal Point could be plainly seen from the ranch. During the second night a wild storm had burst over the crags, obscuring all. There had been no more signals from David, and he had never returned to his little family.

Search parties had gone out to comb the hidden canyons; and a brother had come from the East to follow Daniel's trail, but from that day to this there had been no trace of the lost man, living or dead. He had disappeared as surely as though he had been snatched into outer space. With him had gone the secret of the location of his gold diggings.

As always, when young Dan pondered this ancient family mystery, he became curiously excited, even angry. He longed to charge up those canyons himself, to solve the riddle of the lost man, and to dig the golden secret of the mine from the mountain's very heart.

Others had tried, of course. The story of the Phantom Pony Mine, as it was called, had become a legend in the West. It was as famous as the Lost Dutchman in the Superstition Mountains of Arizona, or the Lost Tayopa of Old Mexico.

The longing for gold had lured many adventurers into

the dangerous canyons during the past seventy-three years. Some had failed to return. None had found the treasure.

But I will! Dan Glover vowed to himself now.

Dan and his sister really lived in the city. Their father was a professor at the university in Tucson. But for many years they had spent their summer vacations on the Bar-Alpha ranch, which still belonged to the daughter of the lost rancher. Not only had they listened countless times to Aunt Charlotte's story of her father's disappearance, but Gordon Halliday, the foreman of the ranch, had fired their youthful imaginations with tales of the lost gold.

Mr. Halliday had promised Dan when he was a small boy that as soon as he was old enough he would take him on an expedition into the mountains to search for the mine.

This was the year. Dan was now fourteen and everything was set for the big adventure. In just a few days—when Mr. Halliday could be spared from his duties at the ranch—they would ride together toward the mountain, taking the same trail that Great-grandfather Glover followed so long ago.

Dan could hardly bear the waiting, and Karen was full of envy. She was not included in the plans, as Aunt Charlotte considered the trip much too hazardous for her. But Dan suspected that she still had hopes of tagging along.

She spoke up suddenly from Dan's side. The thunder had been getting louder by the minute and she had to raise her voice to make herself heard. "Most people think Great-grandfather was murdered by renegade Indians," she said. "But I don't. I think if we looked around up there, we'd find his bones in a canyon. He was probably struck by lightning and fell over a cliff."

"I don't think so," Dan shouted back. "Remember, he was riding. His horse would have come right straight back to the ranch if he had just had an accident, but it didn't. Aunt Charlotte said some old prospector named Tom Weeder rode Daniel's horse into the town of Tombstone days after the disappearance. He said he had traded with an Apache Indian for it, and I think that Indian was responsible for——"

A great clap of thunder drowned Dan's voice. It was so loud that the reverberations rattled the loose stones on the hillside. At the same time, huge drops of rain splashed upon the dusty roadbed. These increased at an alarming rate, and before the young riders could spur their horses on, rain was pouring over them in torrents.

The two horses, Chili and Linda, took their heads and fairly flew in the direction of the ranch. Dan Glover, drenched to the skin and hanging on for dear life, was forced to forget for the moment his dream of searching for the fabulous gold mine.

In only a few moments the boy and girl had reached the ranch entrance. The rain had let up slightly. As Dan jumped down from his horse to open the gate, he chanced to look over his shoulder. There was an unfamiliar car creeping toward him down the road, its headlights glimmering eerily through the blinding downpour.

"Who can that be?" asked Karen.

"I don't know." Waiting until the strange car came to a stop in front of the gate, he handed Chili's reins to his sister and walked toward it.

There were two people in the front seat—a boy and a

woman. As Dan bent to peer inside the car, he got the surprise of his young life. The boy staring out through the window was about Dan's own age, and he was a dead ringer for Dan Glover himself!

There was the same wing of wiry brown hair across his forehead, the same brown eyes and squared-off chin. Of course, the stranger was somewhat thinner than Dan; his skin was fair where Dan's was tanned from the desert sun; and he wore dress-up clothes—a dark tailored suit and black tie.

The boy's resemblance to himself was so powerful that Dan had the uncanny feeling that he was looking at his own ghost. For a moment the boy appeared equally startled. Tardily, he rolled down the car window and spoke.

"How-do-you-do?" he said somewhat stiffly. "We are trying to find the Bar-Alpha ranch."

Ashamed of himself for staring so long, Dan glanced toward the woman who sat behind the steering wheel. She greeted him with a nod.

"Are we on the right road?" she asked. "A man at the junction back on the highway assured us that this was the road to the Glover ranch——"

"Yes, ma'am." Danny found his voice at last. Politely, he touched the brim of his dripping hat. "It's right through this gate, about half a mile up the road.

"My sister and I are on our way to the Bar-Alpha now," he added. "We are spending the summer there with our aunt."

"Oh," the woman smiled delightedly. "Then you must be"—she stopped abruptly and looked past Dan's hat, into the slanting rain—"but we can introduce ourselves later," she added. "You two had better get home and dry off. If you'll just open the gate for us——"

"Yes, ma'am." Dan backed away and ran to unbar the metal gate. He held it open while the car, a green station wagon, passed through.

Karen followed closely, leading Dan's horse, and he quickly locked the gate behind her. As he slipped into the wet saddle once more, he noticed that the green car had an out-of-state license, but he was unable to read it through the rain.

"I didn't know Aunt Chat was expecting company," Karen yelled, as they galloped around a hill in the wake of the strange visitors' car.

"Neither did I," answered Dan gruffly. For some reason, he didn't mention the other boy's odd resemblance to himself. He was a little embarrassed by it.

When Dan and his sister arrived at the sprawling old ranch house, the car was already parked in the front driveway. The two travelers had obviously gone into the the house, for there was no sign of them now.

Chapo Robles, one of the cowhands, scampered out from behind the house and came to take the reins from both Dan and Karen. His old face, lined as a walnut beneath a battered felt hat, was full of kindly concern. He had known the brother and sister from babyhood and always watched out for them.

"I will unsaddle Linda and Chili this time," he offered, as the young riders slipped to the ground. "Is better you go in house and change clothes before you catch the cold."

"Thank you, Chapo," Dan answered gratefully.

He took Aunt Charlotte's mail from the saddle pouch,

and gave his tired horse an apologetic pat on the neck. Then he dashed to join Karen under the shelter of the wide veranda that ran around the house.

It was a rule on the ranch that each rider must unsaddle and brush down his own mount after an excursion. However, Dan felt that they might be forgiven this once for accepting Chapo's help.

Instead of entering the house by the front door, Dan and Karen rounded the corner and climbed an outside stairway to their rooms on the second floor.

Dan wasted no time in changing into fresh jeans and shirt. He even went so far as to wash up and run a comb through his thick hair, out of respect for the visitors. But when he stood in front of the mirror and looked at his familiar, everyday face, he was struck again by his resemblance to the boy in the car. A feeling of uneasiness came over him.

Who was this character in the fancy clothes? he wondered. Why had he come to Arizona? Why, especially, had he come to Aunt Charlotte Glover's remote desert ranch at the foot of Mystery Mountain?

2
The Lost Gold Mine

"Are you ready, Dan?"

Karen appeared in the doorway of Dan's room. She too had cleaned up. Her hair was now neatly combed and she wore a fresh blue dress.

"In a minute."

Dan had paused to glance through the stack of mail he had brought from the mailbox at the highway. He held up a letter addressed in a strange handwriting. It was postmarked Boston, Massachusetts, and Dan glanced at the name in one corner of the envelope.

"Mrs. Robert Grayham," he read slowly. "Does that ring a bell with you, Karen?"

His sister came to look over his shoulder. "No." She frowned thoughtfully. "But we do have some distant relatives back in New England somewhere. I've heard

Daddy talk about them. Oh, come on, Dan," she urged impatiently. "I can't wait to find out what those people are doing at the Bar-Alpha."

Dan gathered up the mail and followed his sister into the hall that led to the stair well. Halfway down the stairs there was a small landing, and the two stood there for a moment, looking curiously down at the scene below them.

This wing of the ranch house had been recently built, and the living room was high-ceilinged and spacious. It had beams of golden Oregon pine, and from one wall projected a massive fireplace of colorful flagstone. Over the polished red tile floors were scattered the bright Indian rugs that Great-aunt Charlotte loved.

Much as Dan admired the huge room, it was not that which now held his attention, but the people in it . . . Great-aunt Charlotte, straight-backed and snowy-haired, was seated in her familiar wheelchair, and on the leather couch opposite her were the newcomers.

"Why, Danny!" Karen gasped. He felt the warm explosion of her breath on his cheek. "That boy looks almost exactly like *you*."

The woman on the couch obviously had the same thought, for she looked up in a startled way as the sister and brother came on down the stairs and into the room.

"I simply can't get over it, Cousin Charlotte," she exclaimed, glancing from Dan to the boy at her side. "These two lads look enough alike to be brothers."

The old lady in the wheelchair smiled. She had the serene eyes and simple dignity of one who has spent a lifetime close to nature, and the sage and sand of the desert were in her speech.

"It's no surprise to me, Marion," she answered crisply.

"Two of their ancestors were identical twins—as like as a pair of matching pistols.

"Dan and Karen, come over here," she called.

They went to stand beside her wheelchair, and Dan put the ranch mail in her lap.

"I want you to meet some cousins of yours from the East," she told them. "This is Marion Grayham and her son, Robert. Robert's great-grandad was the brother of the Daniel Glover who set up this ranch."

"I suppose that makes us third cousins, or something like that," Marion Grayham said with a laugh, as she nodded a greeting to Dan and his sister.

The boy at her side spoke up in a positive tone of voice. "It makes me a third cousin, Mother," he said, "and you are a third cousin once removed, because you are of a different generation from us."

With that, he got to his feet and held out his hand to Dan's sister.

"How-do-you-do, Karen?" he said in his clipped Eastern accent. "I am very glad to know you." He made a small bow in her direction.

Karen was so surprised at this formality from a boy who looked so much like her big, restless brother that all she could do was murmur a shy, giggling, "Hi!"

Then the boy turned to Danny, holding out his hand.

Almost reluctantly, Danny took it. Again he had that strange, spooky feeling at finding himself face to face with this pale likeness of himself. He wasn't sure that he liked the idea. It was almost as if some stranger had stolen his skin and crawled into it.

The other boy appeared equally wary. He started to speak, hesitated, and then with a stiff little nod dropped Dan's hand and returned to his seat on the couch.

His mother smiled at Dan. "Robert and I are just passing through on our way to California," she said. "I am to attend an educational conference there and we couldn't resist the temptation to stop and meet you, since we were so near . . . I did write a letter," she added, "but it must have been delayed——"

"It was in the mail today," said Dan. "It sometimes takes a couple of extra days for letters to get out to the ranch."

"Makes no difference," Aunt Charlotte declared cordially. "Long as you're here, you'll have to spend the night. Dan has an extra bed in his room where Robert can sleep. They'll enjoy getting acquainted."

Speak for yourself, Aunt Chat! Dan came near saying the words aloud. He had an uneasy suspicion that this was more than a casual visit, and at a sudden startling statement from young Robert Grayham he was sure of it.

"The reason I wanted to come to Arizona, Cousin Charlotte," he said, "was to find out about a gold mine that's supposed to be in the mountains around here. My grandfather owned a share of it, and when he died he left his interest to me——"

It was Karen who interrupted. "The Phantom Pony!" she cried. Then she glanced impishly at her brother. "Why, Danny thinks *he* owns that mine. Our great-grandfather found it."

Robert's mother looked somewhat confused.

"Well, the story of a rich gold mine near this ranch has been legendary in our family for years," she explained. "It was my brother's dream, and our father's before that,

24)

but nobody ever took time to come to Arizona to find out about it."

She laughed. "When my stubborn son learned that I was coming west, nothing would do but that he must accompany me and check up on his mine. I warned him that it was probably all a fairy tale."

"But it isn't!" Dan spoke up somewhat heatedly. "There really is gold on Mystery Mountain, isn't there, Aunt Chat?"

The old lady nodded. "There's plenty of it up there," she said, "but nobody knows where it is, any more. When I was a little tyke, my mother had a bag of flaked gold in a secret niche in the wall of our adobe house. My father dug that gold from the hill with his own hands."

"Did my great-grandfather work the mine, too?" asked Robert. There was a burning light in his eyes.

"No," Aunt Charlotte replied. "James Glover—that was your great-grandfather—stayed in the East and taught school. He grubstaked Daniel."

"Grubstaked?" echoed Robert. "What does that mean?"

Dan spoke up. "That means that one brother paid for the food and equipment so that the other one could go prospecting for gold or silver. When they made a strike, they went halves."

"That's right," said Aunt Charlotte. "The Glover twins were partners. They were very close, and when they were boys they talked in a secret language that no one else understood. They even dressed alike. Karen"—she turned to the girl, who now sat on a stool by the fireplace—"go bring me that picture from the wall above my bed."

Charlotte Glover's room was on the ground floor, and it was only a moment before Karen was back with a

(25

photograph in an antique gilt frame. At her aunt's bidding, she handed it to Cousin Marion.

Dan walked around the couch to gaze over his cousin's shoulder. He had seen the picture countless times, yet it always fascinated him.

Two young dandies in the cutaway coats and wide ties of a different era stood side by side. They had identical mustaches and identical watch chains, and each held a cane in a gloved hand.

"That picture was taken soon after they came over from England," said Aunt Charlotte. "The one on the left is Daniel. He gave up prospecting finally, got married and took up this ranch land near the mountain. Then"— she chuckled softly to herself—"by sheer accident he discovered the Phantom Pony.

"He was roaming in the hills one day, when the wind blew the hat from his head. When he went looking in the canyon for it, there it was, hanging from an outcropping of gold quartz!"

"Boy!" exclaimed Robert. And Danny felt the old excitement rise within him. Then he sighed ruefully.

"If only Great-grandfather hadn't gone and got himself lost or murdered or something up on the mountain, we might all be rich."

"Yes," Aunt Charlotte nodded. "Just a few weeks after he made his discovery, he disappeared. It was on a night like this."

Dan lifted his face, listening. He had almost forgotten the storm raging outside. Now he shivered with the others at the sound of the wind screeching through the trees and the cold splash of rain on the tiles of the porch.

Aunt Charlotte's voice broke the spell. "Unfortunately,

my father never filed a claim to the mine, and he never told a soul where it was."

"But he did leave a map," Dan reminded her. He had seen the faded map many times, in the old black chest in the storeroom.

"Yes," she agreed, "he left a map, and plenty of fortune hunters have tried to follow it, but it's full of red herrings. I always figured it was a practical joke of my father's— to put claim jumpers off the trail."

"But I have a map, too!"

Young Robert spoke up suddenly. Jumping to his feet, he faced the others. "It was with the papers my grandfather gave me when he signed over his share of the mine to me. He claimed his father told him that if he could decipher it, it would lead him to a fortune in gold."

Dan Glover felt his heartbeat quicken. "Where is it?" he demanded. A wild idea had struck him.

"It's in my suitcase in the car," the other boy answered. "May I go get it, Mother?" he asked.

"Yes, of course."

By now Karen, too, was on her feet, following the two boys in their dash for the door.

"Get some raincoats," Aunt Charlotte yelled after them. But the three were too excited to worry about something as unimportant as getting wet.

Dan couldn't wait to see Robert's map. Perhaps the two maps went together. This one might be the key that would decipher the old document in the chest.

3

Trails to Treasure

"There it is!"

Importantly, Robert Grayham opened his map on the library table, at one end of the big room. It was yellowed with age and frayed at the edges. The parchmentlike paper crackled as he spread it out, and three eager young faces bent over it.

Against a roughly drawn profile of Mystery Mountain was sketched the trail to the Phantom Pony Mine. Frowning with concentration, Dan moved his finger along the broken line.

"The trail begins here," he stated, "at the Bar-Alpha. There's Signal Point, where Daniel Glover spent his first night. Here's Sombrero Butte, the Needle . . ."

Slowly, he shook his head. "I'm afraid it's just another copy of the one we already have, Robert," he said dejectedly.

28)

Robert's triumphant look faded.

"Of course, I can't be really sure till we compare them," Dan added. "There might be something new in this one. . . ."

"Let's go check right away," suggested Karen impulsively. "Aunt Charlotte," she called to her aunt, who was chatting with Robert's mother, "may we go to Old House and look in the chest?"

Aunt Charlotte glanced up tolerantly. "Run along, if you like," she said. "But watch out for scorpions, and don't stay over there too long. We'll have an early supper tonight. Chavela is making your favorite food—hot tamales and frijoles." Chavela was the plump, black-eyed cook who pampered them all.

The original dwelling at the Bar-Alpha ranch—Old House, as it was now called—was connected with the present wing by a short, open passageway. While the new house was built of burned adobe and was modern in every way, Old House was of frame, with high Victorian windows and wide wooden porches.

Except for the first floor, where Gordon Halliday and his ranch hands had their quarters, the house was vacant. However, one big upstairs room was still used for storage.

"Where is this mine supposed to be?" Robert asked, looking off toward the hills, as he followed Karen and her brother through the arcade between the buildings.

Dan pointed off to the north. "Up there somewhere."

The rain had almost ceased, and except for one distant peak, the mountain was shrouded in blackening shadows. But through the clouds one ray from the setting sun reached out and touched that single peak and turned it to smoldering flame.

Robert paused, awed by the sight. "We watched that same pile of rock for miles and miles when we came in today," he remarked.

"Old Mystery is really a range of mountains," Dan told him. "There are thousands of canyons up there, and places where white men have never set foot."

They hurried on then, anxious to compare their maps, and were soon climbing the stairway to the second-floor storeroom.

Dan pulled the chain of a wall fixture and a light flashed on, revealing a clutter of boxes, trunks and old furniture. Everything appeared to be dripping with cobwebs and Karen made a wry face.

"Spooky in here," she remarked.

Even Robert seemed fussy about getting tangled in cobwebs. So Dan himself went to the corner and pulled out the old chest that had once been brought from England by Daniel Glover. It was black and warped, about the size of a modern foot locker, and strapped with ribbons of tarnished brass.

The chest was unlocked, the key having been long lost, and Dan jerked up the lid, letting fly a small cloud of dust.

Karen sneezed.

There before them was all that remained on the ranch of the effects of the lost adventurer: a couple of old leatherbound hooks, a notebook with faded inscriptions, a goldheaded cane, and several rough chunks of whitish rock with black streaks through it. In a round metal tube was a roll of parchment—Daniel's original map.

Dan's fingers shook a little as he drew out the roll. He always had the strange feeling that the first Daniel's ghost

might be looking over his shoulder when he delved into the old chest. Robert had brought along his own map, and the two boys went to the light, holding the documents side by side.

For a long moment there was silence. Again, Dan shook his head. "There isn't much difference," he said. "I didn't think there would be. After all, if James Glover had had an easy map to the mine, he'd have gone there himself, when he came to Arizona to search for his twin."

"I suppose so." Robert was slightly flushed, frowning. "But why would Daniel give his own brother a map he couldn't follow? Unless——"

He was still staring intently at his map. Suddenly, an exclamation burst from his lips.

"Look!" he cried, pointing to some strange characters scratched above each point marked on the yellowed paper. "Mine is different! Those are Greek letters. See? Alpha, Beta, Gamma—what does that mean?" he demanded.

"I don't know," said Dan shortly. He had vaguely wondered about the letters himself, but he hadn't thought them important, and he had not known that they were Greek. He was somewhat annoyed at finding Robert one jump ahead of him.

"Do you know what I think?" said the other boy. "I think these letters are part of a code. This map is no good by itself. It needs a key to decipher it."

"But if the two brothers had had a code, wouldn't James have had the key?" Dan's sister entered the conversation from another corner of the room. She had overcome her distaste for cobwebs and was rummaging through a big trunk. She looked up at the boys.

"Maybe not," said Robert. "Perhaps Daniel meant to

give James the key and just didn't have a chance. Remember, he didn't expect to be lost on the mountain. . . . Perhaps the key is hidden."

He returned to the old chest.

"What's in that notebook?" he asked.

Dan shrugged. "That's just an old Latin copybook. The brothers were both teachers, you know. There's nothing there. My dad went through all that stuff when he was in college."

Robert had picked up the two leatherbound books and was riffling through the pages. "*A Greek History,*" he read the titles aloud, "and *Plutarch's Lives for Boys and Girls.* Would Cousin Charlotte mind if I took these back to the other house?"

"It's all right, I guess." Robert could waste his time looking at musty old books if he wanted to, thought Dan, but it wouldn't do him much good. In the past seventy years countless people had tried to break the mystery of the lost mine.

"I'm going to stick to the map," Dan said almost defiantly. "There are a lot of odd rock formations on Mystery Mountain and I think it's just a matter of finding the right landmarks. Mr. Halliday, our foreman, has some theories about the map, too. He's going to take me up there soon and——"

The minute he had let the information out, he was sorry. Robert's head jerked up like an alert young buck's.

"When?" he demanded.

"Next week," Dan admitted reluctantly. "Mr. Halliday has been promising me for a long time. But it's a rugged trip," he added hastily. Not for a tenderfoot, he almost added. "Some places are so rough, even a horse can't take them."

The other boy didn't reply, but his young chin, so nearly a match for Dan's, set in a determined line.

Dan tossed his own map into the old chest and closed it with a bang. "Quit meddling in that old junk, Karen, and come along," he said sharply to his sister.

The girl had been examining the outmoded dresses in one of the trunks and she looked up, startled at his voice.

"You needn't be so cross about it," she retorted.

"I'm sorry," Dan said lamely, suddenly ashamed of his show of temper, and of his strange antagonism toward his newly met cousin.

He didn't quite understand it himself. After all, it wasn't Robert's fault that he had Dan's features. Nor could he be blamed for his interest in the Phantom Pony Mine. He had as much right to search for it as anyone.

And the boy was friendly enough, even if he was somewhat of a know-it-all. Still, Dan had the unhappy feeling that this unexpected cousin was going to foul up all his plans, and he followed Robert and Karen down the stairs in a strained silence.

In the lower hall, they met Gordon Halliday, coming from his rooms. He was a tall man in his forties, with graying hair and blue eyes narrowed from long years of gazing toward sunlit desert horizons. He had that proud, owner-of-the-world stride of the true Westerner.

He greeted the young visitor from the East with a pleasant "How-do?" and the question "Is this your first visit to the desert, Robert?" He showed no surprise at the close resemblance of the two cousins.

"Yes, sir," Robert responded with an eager smile. "But not my last, I hope. I'd like to live in Arizona."

At dinner that evening the conversation turned naturally to tales of lost mines, of gold and silver seekers who had disappeared into the far reaches of western mountains and never been seen again, and of Indian lore—for this had been the land of the Apache, the fierce raiders who had resisted the white man for so many years.

"I can see that you two boys have the gold fever bad," remarked Mr. Halliday, from one end of the long table. "How about it, Dan—are you all set to rare up old Mystery to claim your mine?"

"Yes, sir," Dan said, in a low voice.

He didn't look up from his plate. He had had his gear ready for days. His bedroll was laid out in one corner of his room with his mess kit on top. His hunting knife was honed to an invisible edge. He could jump on his horse in ten minutes and be off. But he didn't want to talk about it with Robert sitting beside him.

Robert, however, was already getting into the act. "When do you plan to leave, Mr. Halliday?" he asked eagerly.

"Well, I figure we could get off about day after tomorrow," he answered, smiling at Dan. "I want to help Chapo and the boys move part of the herd down to the south range—there's plenty of water there now since the rains. Then I'll be free to go prospecting——"

"Why can't I go along with you, too?" Robert burst out boldly. "Mother"—he looked at her across the table—"you'll be in California for at least two weeks. Why can't I stay here on the ranch and join the expedition into the mountains? If it's all right with Cousin Charlotte, of course," he added quickly, turning to the old lady who sat at the head of her table.

For a moment there was complete silence. Charlotte Grayham's eyes were troubled.

"I don't know, Robert," she said. "That old mountain is treacherous even for experienced mountaineers. Dan himself has never been beyond Signal Point and he's been climbing rocks all his life. What do you think, Gordon?"

The foreman of the Bar-Alpha shook his head, frowning. He looked intently at the pale, intense face of the Eastern boy.

Robert's longing was so powerful that Dan could feel the pressure of it on the air. He slowly clenched his fist in his lap.

"Can you ride a horse, son?" Mr. Halliday asked, then.

Robert flushed. "Not very well, Mr. Halliday," he admitted honestly. "I've just ridden a little around the park at home. But I can learn," he declared positively. "I can learn to do anything I make up my mind to!"

"Well"—the man took a bite of savory tamale and slowly chewed it before he went on—"it does seem a shame to come way out to Arizona with a paper showing you own half interest in a gold mine, and not even get a chance to look for it.

"I suppose we could put the trip off a couple of days— while you get used to the sun and saddle. That is, if your ma says you can go. How about that, Danny-boy?"

His gaze met Dan's. There was both understanding and challenge in the foreman's eyes. "Could you teach your cousin to stick to a saddle and climb a cliff in the next few days?"

There was a lump as big as a cactus apple in Danny's throat. But he swallowed it gamely.

"I'll do my best Mr. Halliday," he said.

4
Brains from Boston

The next morning, as soon as Karen and the two boys had seen Cousin Marion's green station wagon disappear over the hill in the direction of California, they headed for the corral.

Robert Grayham was about to get his first lesson in western horsemanship. He'd find it wasn't quite as simple as jogging around a bridle path in Boston, thought Danny darkly.

Dan was still unhappy over the turn of events and the postponement of his long-planned trip to Mystery Mountain.

Chapo, the kindly old man who had lived on the Bar-Alpha ranch all his life, met them at the stable. He had brought three horses into the corral. Linda, Karen's little mare, was already saddled.

At the sight of the two boys side by side, Chapo's black eyes crinkled with delight. "*Cuates!*" he cried, looking from Dan to Robert and back again.

The strange word meant "twins" in Spanish and Robert quickly caught on, for he laughed. "We're really distant cousins," he explained. He was now wearing a striped T-shirt and a pair of Dan's blue jeans, and looked more than ever like the Arizona boy.

"Mr. Halliday go down to south range early this morning," Chapo was saying to Dan. "He say let new boy ride your horse, Chili. You ride Flecha today."

"That's great!"

Dan's spirits rose instantly. Flecha, named for the arrow, was the personal property of Gordon Halliday. He had the blood of thoroughbreds and was almost a hand taller than the sturdy little quarter horses usually employed on the ranch. He was wind-fast and graceful, and Dan always thrilled at the chance to ride the foreman's horse.

"Boy, what a beauty!" Robert watched enviously as his cousin brought up a saddle and tossed it expertly across Flecha's back, securing it with a few deft movements.

"Now see if you can saddle Chili," Dan suggested, pointing to his own saddle, which Chapo had placed against the corral.

Willingly, the other boy picked it up and shoved it awkwardly onto the smaller horse. Chili moved sideways and pawed the earth. Dan had to step up and smooth the blanket and help fasten the straps.

Karen was already mounted, trotting back and forth—eager for the morning ride. Soon all three were on their way. Dan led, striking east toward the arroyo that cut through the valley where much of the ranch lay. The desert air was fresh and sweet after the rains, and the colorful land shimmered under a turquoise-blue sky.

Dan glanced back at Robert. He saw that the other boy was sitting the saddle fairly well and that the patient Chili seemed undisturbed at carrying a strange rider. That was at least encouraging.

Dan had been riding horses since he could walk. It seemed a little foolish to him that anyone had to "learn" to ride, and he couldn't help feeling somewhat superior to his young cousin.

Now and then, both Dan and Karen called out bits of advice to Robert: "Keep your heels down." "Don't grip the reins so tight." "Relax!"

"Did you ever hold a little bird in your hand?" Dan asked the other boy, checking Flecha while Robert moved up alongside him. "That's the way you should hold the reins when you're riding slowly like this. Light and easy —except when you're giving your horse commands."

They rode in and around the valley most of the morning. Dan and Karen were proud of the Bar-Alpha and wanted to show it off.

First, they led Robert to the site of the adobe hut, where Daniel Glover had left his family waiting when he took his last, fatal trip into Mystery Mountain. Nothing remained now but a pile of rubble, for wind and rain had broken down the mud bricks long ago, and the timbers had been carried off for firewood.

From behind that spot, they climbed an easy trail to a rocky lookout and turned to gaze back over the distant ranges of the ranch.

"There's Mr. Halliday," cried Karen, pointing to the

(39

south, where six men on horseback herded a bunch of cattle toward a cone-shaped hill, blue in the distance.

"The Bar-Alpha ends beyond that peak," said Dan. "We have over one hundred thousand acres of range land."

"Wheeoooo!" Robert gave out an awed whistle. "Wish my great-granddaddy had been the one to come west," he remarked with a grin. "You're lucky to get to come here summers."

The Eastern boy seemed fascinated by everything on the ranch. He asked a dozen intelligent questions about the West, some of which Dan himself couldn't answer. And he knew a lot—even scientific names for some of the desert plants, and facts about the Indians of the early days.

At one point, the three riders dismounted to examine some small, squarish pits in the ground. They were caved in, but had once been neatly lined with rocks. As Robert approached, a bright orange and black snake slithered out of one of the holes and crawled in front of him.

Dan smiled, expecting the boy to jump back. But instead, Robert watched the creature with delight. "That must be a king snake," he declared. "They're harmless, aren't they?"

Dan nodded. "These pits," he said importantly, "were probably made by the Apaches. They've always been on the ranch, but nobody knows for sure what they were used for."

Robert was down on his knees, frowning, as he examined the hole. "They were probably used for storing food—dried fruits and edible stalks from the century plant, perhaps. Of course, as you know, when wild fruits and game were scarce, the Apaches raided villages of other tribes.

"The squaws dug these pits to store the extra food, and camouflaged them so that they couldn't be found," he added.

Dan glanced at his sister and found her gazing in wide-eyed admiration at her cousin.

"Well, I don't know about that," he said shortly. "But I do know the Apaches raided ranches around in here in the early days, and——" He turned to look up at Mystery Mountain, which was never far from his thoughts. "I've always thought the Apaches attacked my great-grandfather up there. It might even have been old Geronimo himself," he said recklessly, mentioning the famous Chiricahua Apache who had so long resisted the white man in Arizona.

The other boy stood up, dusting off his knees. "Couldn't have been Geronimo," he said pleasantly. "Daniel Glover disappeared in 1889 and it was before that—let me see—it was in 1886 when Geronimo surrendered to General Cook and was sent to Florida."

At that, Danny simply walked away and remounted Flecha. His cheeks were hot beneath the tan. It was bad enough to have this interloper on the ranch at all, but for him to show Dan up for an ignoramus in his own land was hard to bear. . . . Yet Dan knew it was his own fault. He knew the history of Geronimo's bloody raids and the story of his capture well, but as usual, he was hazy about dates.

From then on, Dan rode ahead, broodingly silent, while Karen and Robert came along happily behind him, laughing and joking as though they had known each other always.

After four hours of riding, the Eastern boy was glad to head for the ranch and lunch.

He was stiff and aching when he dismounted from his horse, but he insisted upon following Dan's and Karen's example as they unsaddled and went through the routine of currying Flecha and Linda, and of giving them water and oats.

Robert even refused Chapo's offer of help, and Danny felt a reluctant admiration for the boy. He smiled a little to himself, though, when Robert went limping toward the ranch house, tenderly rubbing the seat of his jeans.

"He'll be plenty sore tomorrow," Dan remarked to Karen.

She flung up her small chin. "Well, I think Robert is doing just fine, smarty," she said in quick defence. "You're miffed because he is cleverer than you."

"Who says so?" Dan retorted. "Just because he reads a lot of books——"

"Well, you'd make better grades in school if you read more," Karen declared, scampering off to join the other boy.

Dan smarted under that thrust. It was an arrow striking home. He had failed in History last year because he had neglected his study.

It wasn't that Dan Glover was dumb. He did all right in the I. Q. department, and he was a whiz in the subjects that came easy, like Algebra and Science. But History required so much reading.

Naturally, Professor Glover, Dan's dad, wasn't pleased about that failing grade. At first he had insisted that Dan go to summer school, but when Dan anxiously reminded him that this was the Big Year—the year Mr. Halliday was to take him to search for the lost mine on Mystery Mountain—the professor had relented. Dan had been allowed to visit Aunt Charlotte, but only on condition that at the ranch he spend an hour or two every day boning up on his history.

Dan obeyed the rule dutifully. Every day after lunch he went to his room and studied. But he still couldn't see the sense in it all. Why should he spend his time learning a lot of dull, dead facts of history when he just wanted to be a rancher and help run the Bar-Alpha?

"In these days, with scientific breeding and feeding, even a rancher needs a good education, Dan," his father had insisted. "Life on earth has become pretty complicated," he had added, "and if a fellow wants to lead a full and useful life today, he's wise to learn all he can—including the lessons of history." But Dan couldn't see it.

When he had washed and gone down to the kitchen, he found Robert and Karen already at the table. Chavela, her round face beaming, was filling their bowls with her famous vegetable soup. Dan couldn't help noticing that his double from the East was charming even the cook with his fancy manners and eager mind.

"This is wonderful, Chavela," Robert declared, after tasting the steaming broth. "What do you call it?"

The woman's brown eyes beamed with pleasure. "*Sopa de verduras,*" she said in her swift soft Spanish.

"Soup-a de ver—ver——"

Verdooooooras," Karen broke in helpfully, drawing out the long "u" sound. "And sopa—not soup-a."

Robert tried again. "Sopa de verdoooooras," he repeated carefully. Both Karen and Chavela laughed with delight.

"You do fine," cried the little cook. "Soon he speak good

Spanish, eh Danny?" She placed a bowl of soup and a glass of milk in front of Dan, but her smile was for the other boy.

Dan ate in silence, taking no part in the cheerful banter, feeling strangely left out. . . . Later, when he went up to his room and propped himself against his pillows to study, his cousin followed, like an unwelcome shadow.

Robert took off his shoes and neatly folded down the coverlet before he stretched himself out on the other twin bed.

"Boy, I'm beat!" he remarked frankly. "Riding a horse is hard work when you aren't used to it. But it was great fun," he added. "Life on a Western ranch is exactly as I pictured it."

Dan mumbled something, trying to keep his attention on Chapter Ten of his *American History.* He hid the cover against his knees so the other boy wouldn't see that he was reviewing a school text.

Robert seemed to think it was perfectly natural to be wrapped up in a book, and when Danny showed no inclination to carry on a conversation, he himself started to read. He took up one of the old volumes he had found in the storeroom the day before, *The History of Greek Civilization,* and was soon lost in its pages. Occasionally, he would chuckle out loud, and sometimes he became so enthusiastic he had to share his thoughts.

"Some of those ancient Greeks were pretty smart, weren't they?" he remarked. "You know who Archimedes was, don't you, Dan?"

"Archimedes?" Dan glanced up to meet his cousin's eager, intelligent eyes. The name drew a faint spark from

(45

his memory. "Wasn't he an—an inventor or something?" he answered, frowning.

"He sure was! He's the old guy who discovered the principle of specific gravity while soaking in the bathtub. It tells you about it here. Listen to this."

He read aloud from the book in his hands:

> "King Hiero II had given his crownmaker a specific amount of gold to make him a new crown. The finished crown weighed the same as the gold, but the king feared that the crafty goldsmith had substituted a portion of silver for some of the gold. To make sure, he called upon Archimedes to test the crown.
>
> "The only known way to make the test was to melt the crown, divide the elements and weigh the gold— but that would destroy the crown. . . . Archimedes was sore pressed to solve the problem, until one day, while getting into his bathtub, he noticed how the water rose around him. In a trice the solution burst upon him and he cried: '*Eureka* . . . I have found it.'
>
> "He filled a container to the brim with water and suspended the crown in it—catching that water which overflowed. Knowing that the displaced water had the same volume as the crown, he obtained an equal portion of gold, and checked its weight against the weight of Hiero's crown. It weighed more than the crown, which proved that the crownmaker had stolen some of the gold. Whereupon the man was found guilty and was executed."

"Pretty clever." Dan laughed. In spite of his annoyance, he had become fascinated with the story, and suddenly, the figure of the ancient scientist, just a vague name from history to him before, became startlingly real. He could

46)

picture the old Greek sitting in his bathtub, pondering his problem. He could almost hear him shout the famous cry: *Eureka!*

Dan had often heard people use that expression, half in jest, when they made a sudden discovery, but it took on new meaning now that he knew the origin of it. Other bits of information about Archimedes floated up into his mind.

"Wasn't he the man who first suggested controlled missiles in warfare?" he asked.

"I think so." Robert leafed back through the book.

From the discussion of the ancient problem-solver and his amazing inventions, the boys' talk turned naturally to the subject of guided missiles and modern space travel. Dan could hold his own, now, and for a little while he forgot that his present companion was the "bottleneck" that held up his golden adventure—the rediscovery of the Phantom Pony mine.

He was reminded of it soon enough, however. Karen appeared at the door, freshly bathed and dressed, and begged Robert to join her downstairs in a game of croquet, pointedly ignoring her brother. However, Robert begged Dan to join them. "You can play off the winner," he suggested.

Dan refused. "I want to finish my chapter," he said. But after they had gone, he let the book fall shut against his knees and gazed gloomily through the window.

His room faced to the north, and there, bulking blue against the desert sky, Mystery Mountain waited. . . . The days of opportunity were slipping by. Summer vacation on the Bar-Alpha ranch would soon be over.

5
Double Trouble

"It's going to be rougher today," Dan warned his cousin, as the two boys once more rode off in the early morning sun, followed by Karen on the pinto. "We'll take an old Indian trail up to Victory Pass, so you can get some practice riding in the canyons."

He pointed to a V-shaped cut against the horizon in the hills to the east.

"There's a beautiful view of the valley from there," Karen told Robert, coming up beside them, "and some prehistoric rock forts built by the Indians. Dan and I found arrowheads up there. . . ."

Dan gave Flecha a light prod and galloped on ahead, because he didn't feel in the mood for talk. He couldn't help thinking that he might have been riding toward Mystery Mountain to search for the old mine, if it hadn't been for Robert.

48)

As he had promised, the trail soon became rough. It wound narrowly about the edge of cliffs and plunged in and out of scrub oak canyons. Robert must have been a little nervous at times, but he made no protest and came doggedly on, a few paces behind Karen's horse.

The sun blazed high in the sky when they finally reached Victory Pass and, tying their horses below, climbed up to the rocky cut. They ate their lunch there, and from where they sat they could look for miles away in both directions. Almost the whole Bar-Alpha ranch spread below them to the west, while to the east, covering the hills as thick as grass, were thousands of giant saguaros, the spiny ancients of the desert.

Chavela had packed sandwiches and fruit for them, and each had brought a canteen of cool water. Dan ate as hungrily as the other two, and after lunch he joined them in their search for Indian relics behind the crude rock walls that partly encircled the slope below the divided peak.

"The Apaches used to hide behind these forts," explained Karen, "and exchange arrows with invading tribes."

They searched the ground in vain, however, and Robert finally gave up. "Wish I could have found a couple of arrowheads at least," he said in some disappointment. "I'd sure like to take something back to show the fellows at home."

"Maybe we'll have better luck down in the valley," remarked Karen. "Small ones often wash out of the ground with the rains, but they aren't too easy to find. I'd give you some of mine," she added generously, "but I let Daddy put them all in the museum at his university.

"Dan has a big collection of his own back at the ranch, though," she added mischievously, looking straight at her brother.

"They're mostly bird points," Dan said gruffly. "Those were used by the Indians for hunting small game." But he didn't find himself making any noble gestures just then. He was proud of that collection. "We'd better start back," he said instead, leading the way toward the horses.

As they walked behind him, Karen and Robert continued their conversation, turning naturally from Indian artifacts to speculation about what happened to Daniel Glover and the lost mine.

"Dan says an Indian might even have used a bow and arrow to shoot Great-grandfather Glover," she stated seriously. "Chapo Robles has lived around here for over sixty years and an old Indian woman told him that the gold on Mystery Mountain was sacred to the Apache Thunder God. She said when white men disturbed the gold up there, the god sent bolts of lightning to stop them."

Robert laughed. "That's just an old superstition, of course. The modern Indians are probably too busy watching television to worry about lost gold mines. I doubt if we meet any vengeful Apaches, or any Thunder Gods either, when we go after the gold."

At that bold statement Dan turned his head and glanced at his cousin. "Don't be so sure about that, Rob," he said. "Just a couple of years ago a prospector from Phoenix was found dead in a canyon up there. They never did find out what happened to him."

Robert's confidence annoyed Dan. He seemed so sure that with the aid of his magic map and a few miracles he could gallop up old Mystery and walk right into a canyon of gold! Although Dan himself had harbored the same wild and hopeful dream for years, he was beginning to have vague misgivings about the whole project.

The ride homeward was over the familiar trail, and Dan soon became weary of being overcautious for the sake of the Eastern visitor. By the time he came within sight of the ranch house and the trail had widened, he had become so keyed up that he had to let off steam. He had to show off.

Looking over his shoulder at Karen and Robert, he waved them forward. "Race you to the arroyo!" he shouted. Then, bending his body, he flicked the reins, urging the big stallion to increase his speed.

"Come on, Flecha," he prompted. "Let's show that tenderfoot what real riding looks like."

Flecha was already tired, but thoroughbred that he was, he bounded ahead down the slope. As always when he raced with Flecha, Danny felt a great surge of power go through him. He loved the sense of flying and the staccato music of hoofbeats on the rocky trail. The wind sang past his head, and he leaned forward in the saddle until the blowing mane touched his cheek.

In a few moments he reached the valley floor and soon pulled up beside the arroyo. He turned around to see Karen not very far behind, and got off his horse to wait for her.

"That wasn't fair!" she cried, as she rode up. Her hair was awry and her face flushed. "You not only had a head start on us, but you had the fastest horse."

"It's not the horse that matters, but the rider," Dan answered.

His sister got out of the saddle and slipped to the ground beside him. "I can't understand you, Dan," she said, her voice suddenly worried. "You are always cutting Rob down, and he hasn't done a thing."

Danny flushed at that, but he didn't answer, and they stood side by side, watching Robert come toward them across the valley, the gallant little quarter horse at full speed.

By the time Robert made his belated arrival, Dan had begun to feel a bit guilty.

"I'm sorry, Rob," he said sheepishly, as the other boy slipped from the saddle.

To his surprise, Robert didn't seem to hear. There was no animosity in his face. His eyes were shining and he kept staring, not at Dan, but at Flecha, the big stallion, who had by now wandered down into a puddle in the middle of the arroyo.

"That's some horse!" he declared, wonder in his voice. "I don't think he even touched the ground, coming down that mountain!"

"He's the fastest horse on the ranch," Karen remarked. She sat down in the shade of a mesquite tree, thoughtfully draining the last drop of water from her canteen. Dan joined her, leaning back against the tree trunk, giving all three horses a chance to take a drink and rest. He was totally unprepared for what happened next.

When Flecha finally plodded back up the bank, Robert Grayham dashed forward to meet him, seized the reins in one hand and put his foot in the stirrup, ready to mount!

The startled horse reared a bit, tossing his mane, and Dan and Karen sprang to their feet.

"What do you think you're doing?" Dan cried.

Robert looked around defiantly. "I'm going to ride Flecha back to the house. It isn't far, and I've had enough experience——"

"No!" Dan confronted his cousin, making a grab for the bridle, which the other boy held fast.

"Why not?" demanded the other boy. "You can take Chili from here on. After all, he's really your horse."

"I said no." Karen had come running, to interfere in the quarrel, and Dan held her back with one arm, at the same time giving his cousin a slight shove.

Robert stumbled backward, losing the reins. Suddenly, he burst into anger.

"You don't like me, do you?" he said challengingly. "You've hated me since the night I arrived. You're sore because I own a share of the Phantom Pony——"

"That has nothing to do with it," Dan declared, flushing. "Flecha's a high-strung animal. He isn't used to strange riders. He could throw you and break your neck."

Robert laughed at that. "It's my neck," he said, "and I'm not afraid. You can at least let me try to ride him. It's not fair for you to have the thoroughbred all the time while I have to plug along on that old nag of yours."

He pointed derisively at Chili, who had now come quietly up to Dan's side, as though to back up his young master.

Dan was instantly furious. "Chili's no nag," he retorted hotly. "He's the best quarter horse on the ranch. He— he——"

Dan choked on the words. Sensing Chili's nearness, he turned, to find the horse's brown eyes fixed upon him, soft and adoring and humble. And all at once Dan realized that Robert's frank words held a note of bitter truth. The

(53

horse was tired after the cruel run. His coat still glistened with sweat; his head drooped. Danny saw that Chili was no longer young.

The little horse had been Dan's summer pal on the ranch for as far back as he could remember. Like the best of his breed, he had been quick and agile in cutting the herds, and lightning fast on short runs. Now he was completely outclassed by the younger horse, Flecha.

Unhappily, Dan put his arm across Chili's neck. In his pride in handling Gordon Halliday's horse, he had neglected his own pet.

"You're still the best in my book, Chili," he murmured now, loyally. "Maybe you can't run so fast any more, but you've got more heart than any of 'em."

A shout from Karen and a nervous snort from Flecha caught his attention. Dan jerked his head up to see his cousin once more trying to mount the big horse. Karen had hold of the boy's T-shirt, pulling for all she was worth.

"You're crazy, Rob," she protested. "He's too temperamental. He'll throw you!"

She let go, then, and turned pleadingly to her brother. "Stop him, Dan," she cried. "You know how dangerous it is."

Dan had already started forward. He could have stopped the foolish boy easily enough, but some imp within him suddenly got in the way. *Let him go ahead*, the vengeful imp whispered.

Dan stood still. "Leave him alone, Karen," he said grimly. "Let him learn the hard way."

It didn't take long—or so Dan thought. . . . No sooner had Robert gained the saddle than Flecha reared up and tumbled him off. The bank of the arroyo was soft, and the boy was on his feet in an instant.

Dan and Karen laughed from relief. Then, to their dismay, they saw Robert start again for the horse, which, thoroughly alarmed now, was ambling off to safety.

But somehow the stubborn boy caught up with him, gripped the pommel and shoved himself back into the saddle. This time, however, his seat was faulty and he lost the stirrups completely. The frightened horse made a wild dash toward the hills, with the young rider dangling precariously from his back.

Nearing a huge rock, Flecha made a sudden swerve, and the boy tumbled again to the ground. This time he didn't get up right away.

By now, Dan and Karen were running with desperate speed toward the scene of the accident. When they reached him, Robert was making a valiant effort to sit up. He looked dazed, and there was an ugly scrape on his cheek.

"Are you hurt?" asked Karen. The girl was crying a little.

"I'm not sure." Rob tried to stand, then sank back with a moan of pain. "It—it's my ankle," he gasped. "I think it might be broken."

"Well, stay right there for now," Dan ordered. He wasn't feeling very well himself, just now, but he knew he had to take charge. He looked around. Flecha was long gone, flying off toward the ranch, and the other horses were still at the arroyo. He thought at first of getting Chili and helping Robert into the saddle, but he decided against that. The boy might be badly injured.

"I'll ride to the ranch for help," he said at last. "One of the men can drive the pickup back for you." He looked at his sister. "You stay here with Robert, Karen, and keep him as comfortable as you can."

"Please hurry, Dan." Karen was already on her knees beside the injured boy. She had rolled up her sweater, which she had had tied about her waist, and was now putting it under Rob's head.

"Don't worry." Dan was already on his way toward the horses. He hoped that Chapo or Mr. Halliday would be down at the corral. He was really anxious.

The accident was largely his fault. He should have kept his cousin from taking that reckless ride on Flecha.

6
The Mysterious Clue

"Do you think the bone is broken?"

Dan Glover stood beside Robert's bed, anxiously looking on, as Gordon Halliday bound up the swollen ankle. Robert, still badly shaken, had been carried up to his room and was now resting against the pillows. A square of gauze was plastered over his left cheek.

"Seems to be just a bad sprain," Mr. Halliday replied. "But to be on the safe side, I think you'd better stay off of this foot for today," he told the boy. "If it isn't better in the morning, we'll run you into the city for an X-ray."

He fastened the bandage and then looked up at Dan. His face was serious. "It could have been worse," he said grimly. "I thought you had more sense, Dan, than to let an inexperienced rider take a flighty horse like Flecha."

Dan didn't look at his cousin, but his lips shook a little. "Yes, sir," he said. "I'm sorry, Mr. Halliday."

Then, to his surprise—before the foreman could say anything more—Robert spoke up from the pillow. "It wasn't his fault, Mr. Halliday," he insisted. "Dan tried to keep me from getting on Flecha, but I wouldn't listen to him. We had been racing down the trail, and when I saw how fast the big horse was, I—I just couldn't resist trying to ride him.

"I'd have done it, too," he added stubbornly, "if I hadn't got him all nervous."

Mr. Halliday's gaze never left Dan's face. Unflinching, Dan met it. He had to accept the blame, in spite of Robert's own admissions. First, he had broken a strict rule of the ranch in racing the tired horses; second, he could have prevented Robert from riding Flecha if he had made a real effort.

"I—I suppose this means our trip to Mystery Mountain is canceled," he said to the foreman. "With Robert hurt and all——"

There was a heavy silence. Once more it was Robert who broke it. "No, Dan," he said. "You go along without me. I know I spoiled your plans in the first place, by inviting myself on the expedition. If you wait for me now, you might not have time to search for the mine."

Dan's first reaction was one of relief. Then he made the mistake of meeting his cousin's eyes, and he was lost. The strange twinship they shared was not just a matter of looks. Dan sensed exactly how the other boy felt, and what it cost him to give up the dream.

"Well, how about it, Dan?" Mr. Halliday spoke up. "Do you want to start for the mountain in the morning?"

"No, sir. I'd rather not go till Robert can go with us."

Dan was as surprised as anyone at the words that

came from his lips, and more surprised to know that they were sincere. In spite of the original antagonism for the boy, he realized now that Robert had become part of the big adventure. The search for the mine would be much more exciting, and possibly more successful, with a companion of his own age along.

"After all, Mr. Halliday," Dan added, with a grin for his injured cousin, "we may need those Boston brains of Rob's to help us interpret Daniel Glover's map."

Robert flushed with pleasure. Still, he protested. "What if my ankle really is wrecked for climbing?"

Dan shrugged. "So what if it is? If we can't go this year, we'll plan to meet right here next summer, and search for the mine. But I think the old ankle is O.K. I think in a couple of days we're going to be heading up those canyons to the Phantom Pony."

He stepped up to the bed, and in some embarrassment, held out his hand. "What do you say, Rob, are we real partners?"

The Eastern boy gripped Dan's hand. They not only were partners but were beginning to be friends.

With a satisfied smile, Gordon Halliday slipped unnoticed from the room, while the two boys fell into an animated discussion of strategy for conquering the obstacles on old Mystery.

When their tongues ran down, from sheer expenditure of enthusiasm, Dan reluctantly picked up his *American History* to do his studying, and Robert began to read the book on Greek history that he had taken from Daniel Glover's ancient chest.

The boy had already carefully scanned the margins of the old books for a notation that might give him a clue

60)

for deciphering his map. He had found nothing promising, but being an avid reader, he now became lost in the tales of ancient Greek adventurers and in the fascinating stories of archaic cities.

Robert was still reading when Dan laid aside his history, so Dan picked up the copy of *Plutarch's Lives* that lay on the bedside table and began to leaf idly through it. He still couldn't quite understand why Robert wanted to waste his time with such stuff.

Then, the name of Alexander the Great caught his eye, and before he realized it, he was deep in the story of the famous conqueror's boyhood. He read about Romulus and the founding of Rome, and was fascinated by stories of Lysander, the resourceful naval commandant, who sailed the seas before the time of Christ.

"Boy, those old Greeks and Romans had plenty of answers, didn't they?" he remarked at last in wonder, looking across at his cousin.

Robert put his book aside. "They were smart, all right," he agreed. Then he grinned. "My dad always tells me that the answer to every problem is written somewhere in a book. I just wish these old Greeks would point the way to the Phantom Pony Mine for us."

Karen appeared at the door, bright and sparkling from her day in the open. "Dinner is almost ready," she told the boys. "Chavela wants to know if you want her to send yours up here, Robert."

The boy stretched himself, smiling back at her. "I don't think so. I feel fine," he said. "If Dan will lend me a shoulder to lean on, I think I can hobble downstairs."

So, with Robert hanging onto Dan's shoulder, hopping

on one good foot, the two boys went below, laughing with every step.

As they came into the dining room, Chavela, who was putting salad on the table, looked up. Her round face glowed.

"Cuates!" she cried in delight, just as Chapo had done when he saw how much the two boys resembled each other.

Aunt Charlotte smiled up at them from her wheelchair at the head of the table. "Cuates has two meanings in Mexico," she explained. "It means twins—but it also means pals."

The next day, Robert's ankle was much better. Mr. Halliday examined it and pronounced definitely that no bones were broken.

"The swelling is going down and it will do it good for you to walk around some today," he stated. "I think by tomorrow you'll be back on horseback."

Robert was jubilant. The foot still hurt a little when he put his weight on it, however, and Dan offered to go up on the hill and find a manzanita cane for him to hobble about with.

It was Karen who had the bright idea. "Why not get that old cane out of the storeroom?" she suggested. "I'm sure Aunt Charlotte won't mind."

Their great-aunt willingly gave permission, and Dan himself went to Old House and brought back Daniel Glover's gold-headed cane.

It was made from some shining black hardwood, which Dan thought must be teak. The top half of it was perfectly round and smooth, but the lower part of the tapered

(63

shaft was intricately carved with a design of vines and monkey figures.

"Must be from India," Robert suggested, reaching for the cane.

"Let me see," said Karen eagerly, and before Robert could take it, she had grabbed the walking stick and was strutting around the room with it, like an actor on the stage—showing off in front of her cousin.

Dan was a little annoyed. "Give it here," he demanded, reaching for it as she danced past him. "It's Rob who needs a cane."

He seized the stick, but Karen held on to the knob, laughing, as her brother twisted and pulled. Then she fell back slightly, the gold knob still in her hand!

"Now, look what you've done," Dan said furiously. "You've broken"—he stared down at the black stick—"no, you haven't," he said then, in amazement. "It just came apart, and look! There's a secret compartment in the top of it."

He was holding it out to Robert, much excited now. The gold knob had been screwed to the stick. There was a small opening in the top of the iron-hard cylinder.

"There's something inside!" cried the other boy.

Dan closed one eye and peered into the small compartment. There was a light-colored object inside. He turned the cane upside down, and then tried unsuccessfully to extract it with his fingers. Finally he had to get a pair of tweezers.

By the time he had got the thing out—it turned out to be a narrow, rolled-up piece of paper—all three were shaking with suspense. The paper was yellowed and brittle. Although Dan drew it out to its full length on the library table with the utmost care, he could not avoid tearing the edge.

"It must be the key to the map," Karen whispered from behind his shoulder.

"But there's nothing on it," declared Robert, who, forgetting his injured ankle, had hobbled to join the others.

"Yes, there is!" Dan pointed with excitement at the curly object. "See, there along the edge—those are ink marks. But," he added with a sigh of disappointment, "they don't mean anything. They're not even letters—just scratches."

Rob was bent over, scowling. "They—some of them look like parts of letters," he said, "but it doesn't make any sense."

He looked glumly up at Dan. "If this is really the key to the map, I'm afraid we'll need a key to decipher the key!"

"Let's go ask Aunt Charlotte about it," suggested Karen. "She might remember something that will help."

"Here, Rob." Dan screwed the gold knob back on the walking stick and handed it to his cousin. "Might as well use the cane anyhow," he said.

The three young people found their great-aunt in the kitchen supervising the making of blackberry jam. There was a pan of berries in her lap and she was picking stems from them. She looked up at the three puzzled faces.

"Do you know anything about this, Aunt Chat?" Dan asked, showing her the paper and explaining how they had found it in the gold-headed cane.

The elderly woman looked closely at the strip of yellowed paper, the furrows in her old face deepening.

"Doesn't look like much of anything to me," she stated calmly. "Just some pigeon scratches on paper—or maybe

(65

like it was made by one of those machines in a doctor's office."

"But have you ever seen it before?" Dan demanded, trying to prod her memory.

"Most likely. . . . Remember, that old cane has been around the place for over seventy years. I expect others have discovered that paper and been puzzled about it."

Aunt Charlotte put her pan of berries on the table and leaned against the back of her chair. "I told you James and Daniel Glover had a secret language when they were boys. They probably wrote in code, too——"

"And put messages in their canes," the quick, imaginative Karen broke in, "and then exchanged the canes, and nobody guessed!"

Robert laughed. "They'd have made great undercover agents," he remarked.

By now Aunt Charlotte had closed her eyes. The sunlight coming through the kitchen window made a silver halo of her hair.

"I remember," she said dreamily, "when my uncle James came from the East. I was only a child, but I remember because I thought it was Papa come back to life again.

"Uncle James went up on the mountain to search for his brother. . . . When he came back, he talked and talked to my mother, and they looked for something. They looked in Papa's letters and in the old chest——"

"He was looking for the key to the map that Great-grandfather had sent him," Dan said with conviction. "But it couldn't have been hidden in the cane," he added in a puzzled way, "because that was here all the time."

Aunt Charlotte was almost asleep. Karen kissed her gently on the cheek, and the three slipped away—after robbing a big tray of doughnuts which Chavela had set to cool on the table.

When he went to his room, Dan wrapped the little scroll of paper carefully in a handkerchief and put it safely away in his box of Indian bird points.

The paper was useless, of course. Even Robert, who was fast with the brain work, didn't seem to have the faintest idea how to go about deciphering the scratches. Yet there was something about it that disturbed Dan greatly.

"It's crazy," he said helplessly to Robert, "but I have the strangest feeling that I should know the way to decode that paper and just can't think of it!"

7
On the Trail at Last!

All that night, Dan's dreams were plagued by visions of the curious little coil of paper. It kept unwinding in his mind like a roll of confetti, taunting his memory, but he awoke the next morning as mystified as ever.

Then, in the busy days that followed, he forgot all about it. First, Mr. Halliday himself took the boys for a short jaunt into the hills. He seemed satisfied with Robert's ability to ride and with the boy's confidence in the saddle.

There followed happy hours of preparation, finding a bedroll and other gear for Robert and going to town to buy supplies. All this time Karen, who was usually in the middle of everything the boys did, stayed out of their way. She occupied herself with mysterious deeds in the kitchen; she held secret sessions behind closed doors with Aunt Charlotte; and she made an unusual number of hush-hush calls to her parents in Tucson.

If Dan had not been so occupied himself, he might have suspected his sister's trickery in time to forestall it—for trickery it was. On the evening before their departure, when the two boys dragged their gear down to the porch, Karen finally showed her hand.

There was a sound of thumping and bumping on the outside stairway, and there she was, with her own sleeping bag and a couple of lumpy canvas sacks, all prepared to go along. There was a triumphant gleam in her eyes.

Dan glared at her. "Just where do you think you're going?" he demanded.

"With you and Rob." She grinned at him.

"Oh, no you're not! Mother will never agree to such a silly plan, and neither will Aunt Charlotte. This is going to be a man's trip, rough and hard and no soft stuff. We don't want to be bogged down by any helpless girl. Do we, Robert?" He turned to his cousin.

Robert looked a little helpless himself, in the face of Karen's challenging stare, but he sided loyally with Dan. "That's right," he declared. "No girls allowed."

"Well, I'm not helpless," Karen retorted. "I can ride as well as both of you, and I can do a lot of things that you can't! I can help with cooking, and if people get hurt, I can fix 'em up."

She kicked one of the canvas bags at her feet. "I took a First Aid course with the Red Cross, and I've got my kit right in there. . . . Besides, I've already talked to Mom and Dad about it, and I convinced Aunt Charlotte. They all said I could go along if Mr. Halliday says it's all right."

During this heated discussion the foreman himself had come quietly up onto the porch. Now Dan turned to him.

"And did you say she could come, too?" he asked accusingly.

The foreman nodded. "I told Karen she could join the party on one condition—" he began.

"But why?" Dan felt betrayed. "You made me wait until I was fourteen to take this trip because of the dangers, and Karen is only twelve. It doesn't add up!"

Mr. Halliday looked a little sheepish. He had always been a softy where Karen was concerned. "I suppose you're right, Dan," he admitted. "Some day you'll learn that it isn't always easy to say no to a determined and attractive young lady. But you didn't hear me out. I said that Karen could go along only on one condition, and that is if you say the word. After all, this is your trip, Dan."

Dan flushed and turned away, refusing to meet Karen's eyes. "Well, I won't say the word," he mumbled stubbornly. "She can't go."

Even as he said it, he knew defeat. Karen was beside him in an instant, tugging at his arm. Her eyes weren't defiant and saucy now, but soft and pleading.

"Don't be an old meanie, Dan," she begged. "We've always done everything together before, when we came to the ranch. I promise not to be any bother at all on the trip, and I don't want any of the old gold. I just want to help find the mine. Say yes, Dan."

Dan glanced at Robert, to find him smiling faintly. He knew he was outnumbered. "All right," he said reluctantly. "You win—but you'll have to carry your load all the way."

He turned back to Mr. Halliday. "This makes horses a problem," he said. "Rob is used to Karen's horse."

"He can still ride Linda," the girl offered, happy now that her victory was won. "I can ride one of the range horses."

"That's fine." Mr. Halliday agreed at once. "We'll all

take range horses, then, except Rob. I don't want to risk Flecha on those canyon trails, and old Chili couldn't stand the gaff, either."

Dan agreed somewhat sadly with this decision. He had enjoyed so many adventures along with Chili that he hated to leave his horse behind. However, in the excitement of last-minute planning, his blue mood evaporated. He even got used to the idea of Karen's joining the party.

Mr. Halliday had decided not to take pack animals. "We can cover more ground if we travel light," he had said. "We'll take just what we can carry in our saddlebags and behind us, and we'll count on mountain springs for water."

Robert had all but forgotten his injured ankle, and by the time the four adventurers started up the trail toward Mystery Mountain the next morning, he had little to show for his accident but a healing scar on his cheek.

It was just daybreak. There was a pale, lemon-yellow light behind the mountains to the east and the clouds were edged with gold.

Mr. Halliday led the party, with Karen behind him and Robert following on Linda. Dan brought up the rear, riding tall in the saddle. Jubilation swelled within him until the pressure of it hurt. It seemed as though he had been waiting all his life for this day, and for the opportunity to conquer the mountain.

The first part of the trail was easy to follow; it had been traveled by the prehistoric men of the desert, and by the nomadic Apaches, who had their stronghold in the cliffs above. Dan and Karen had both been over some of the trail, and Gordon Halliday had spent many days prospecting on the mountain during his long years as foreman of the Bar-Alpha.

To young Robert Grayham, however, the experience was completely new and wonderful. He had brought his copy of the old Phantom Pony map along; both he and Dan had pored over it so often that they had almost memorized the landmarks drawn upon it.

"That must be Onka's Leap!" he exclaimed at one place, pointing to a great castellated bluff thousands of feet above and beyond them.

"Yes, it is." Dan was now jogging along beside his cousin, and Karen turned to add her bit to the conversation.

"See that rock beside the castle, Robert—the one that looks sort of like the Statue of Liberty? That represents Onka herself. She was supposed to be a beautiful Indian girl, and——"

"There was a storm on the mountain one night," Dan took up the story, "when the girl was being tracked by some enemy braves. Instead of leading them to her own camp, Onka tricked them by leading them to that precipice. She sacrificed herself by jumping off, and one by one they followed her—plunging to their deaths."

"That's some jump, even for an Indian," Robert remarked with a laugh. But he was properly awed by the legend. "That other peak up there, the one shaped like a hat"—he pointed once more—"that must be the one called Sombrero Butte."

Dan nodded. The eroded peak, with its enormous rounded crown, looked very much like the giant Mexican hat for which it was named. Dan focused his eyes upon it as they rode along for a time in silence.

He had gazed up at the rocky fortresses of Mystery Mountain countless times, but now strangely, with Robert at his side, he felt that he was seeing them all for the first time. He was suddenly dismayed at the enormity of the task that confronted them.

The misty light of morning tinted the mountain with varying shades of blue. The peaks and canyons blended one into another, stretching on and on beyond his sight. Mr. Halliday had once remarked that it would take a lifetime to explore all those hills and valleys.

How, then, could they even hope to find the mute remains of one small human being in all that vastness? How could a person follow a trail that was cold now after seventy years?

For some time the riders traveled through the desert terrain of the foothills. They crossed through thickets of mesquite and green-trunked palo verde trees, and passed clumps of ocotillos with their thorny, whiplike branches. Occasionally, to Robert's delight, a shy Harris squirrel scurried through the brush. Once, he sighted a covey of beautifully marked quail and ordered the party to stop while he watched them rise up and take off, topknots waving.

"Gambel's quail!" he shouted. "I've seen pictures of them, and I'd know them anywhere."

As the sun mounted in the sky, the four riders climbed higher into the mountains, and were soon in the chaparral regions. The trail snaked around the edges of cliffs and led in and out of canyons thick with scrub oak and piñons. It had narrowed so that they were once more forced to ride single file.

In spite of the higher elevation, the sun beat, heavy

(73

and hot, on their backs, and Dan was grateful when Mr. Halliday finally reined in his horse and dismounted.

"We'd better take a break here, Dan," he shouted back, "and have some lunch."

It was just a short climb down to a pleasant spot in a narrow canyon. There were silvery pools of water from the recent rains, and the party staked their horses where they could drink and forage in the grass. Then Karen surprised them all by reaching into one of the lumpy bags she had brought along and producing a bonanza of delicious food.

"Boy, this is the life!" remarked Robert, relaxing under a tree while she spread the feast before them. "Fried chicken, rolls, cookies—wow! I was all set to break out the canned beans and hardtack."

Karen beamed. "Aren't you all glad I came along? I made the cookies myself," she said proudly.

"Looks good, all right," Dan admitted, reaching for a piece of the chicken. "That riding sure makes you hungry."

"Better eat hearty, boys," Mr. Halliday advised, with a laugh. "This may be the last civilized meal we'll have for some time. From now on, it'll be woodsmen's rations, I'm afraid."

While they ate their fill, Dan looked thoughtfully around him. This spot had probably been like this for centuries. "I wonder if Great-grandfather Glover ever stopped here," he said.

Halliday shrugged. "¿Quien sabe?" he replied. "Who knows? Tonight we'll be sleeping near Signal Point, just as Daniel did on his first night out, and by tomorrow night we'll reach the last place he was known to have been alive. It is a spot called Coffee Pot Hill. All theories about his disappearance begin and end there."

(75

"Why is it called that?" asked Robert. "Is there a hill there shaped like a coffee pot?"

The man shook his head. "No," he said gravely. "When the first search party that followed Dan Glover's trail reached that spot they found his coffee pot. It had been turned over on the ashes of his campfire. . . . They figured Daniel had been surprised there and had left in a hurry. But that's where the trail ends and the riddle begins."

They had finished their repast by now, and Karen, like a dutiful little housekeeper, was burying the trash in a hole scooped out by Robert with his hatchet.

Dan stood. "Hurry up," he urged impatiently. He knew that there was still a whole day and a half of hard riding before them, yet he felt a terrible impatience to reach the spot called Coffee Pot Hill.

8

The Needle's Eye

It was still daylight when Signal Point came once more into view. Mr. Halliday selected a camp site in a sheltered spot near a clearwater spring, and his three young companions began to set up camp for the night.

When Karen began to tug at her bedroll and had a bit of trouble dislodging it, the gallant New England boy sprang forward to help her. Dan put a heavy hand on his shoulder.

"Oh, no, Sir Galahad," he said with a grin. "Karen does her own chores just like the rest of us. Let her learn the hard way. We've got to rustle up wood for the fire."

"Take only dead wood," Mr. Halliday called after them, as the boys took off. "There's plenty of it and we don't want to destroy live trees."

As the sun went down, the air in the canyon became

chilly and the boys sat enjoying the warmth of the fire they had made, while Mr. Halliday made camp biscuits and Karen heated their beans and ham. Karen got smoke in her eyes and soot on the end of her small nose, but even Dan admitted that she was game and complimented her on the tasty supper.

"That's where the Apache Indians held out for so long," he said to Robert, gesturing with his fork toward Signal Point. "They hid among the rocks up there and they weren't exactly friendly. . . . Anybody coming up the trail was a perfect target for an arrow through the heart."

Robert sucked in his breath, but he remained silent. Dan, watching the shadows on the cliffs that rose behind the Point, thought for a moment he had seen something move there. It was only his imagination, of course, but the figure of an Indian boy, with a band around his long black hair, had seemed to flit among the rocks and vanish in the shadows.

Before they crawled into their bedrolls that night for a few hours of well-earned rest, the two boys and Karen climbed up onto the great butte and built a signal fire. Aunt Charlotte, at the Bar-Alpha ranch below, saw it and answered with Chapo's powerful flashlight.

The next day's journey was much the same. There were canyons, one after another, to traverse, varied at times by pleasant treks across tree-covered hillsides. The aspen trees in some places were changing color; their round leaves quivered like golden coins in the sunlight. The air was scented sweetly with cedar and pine.

At one time Robert swore that he saw a mountain lion sneak across the cliff above them, but the others could not spot it. Late in the afternoon, the party came unexpectedly upon a mountain meadow, where half a dozen small whitetail deer were browsing.

They watched the shy animals for fully ten minutes before the deer suddenly caught the man-scent and bounded into the woods. It was soon after this that Mr. Halliday led the boys to a high spot and pointed to a stark bluff of decomposed granite, lying to the east.

"Just below that," he informed them, "is Coffee Pot Hill."

Dan was weary from the day's ride, but now, in his eagerness to reach his destination, he forgot his aching shoulders and back. He was glad to find that the rest of the trail was fast and easy.

In a very short time they were dismounting on an exposed tableland, from which the hill sloped easily downward to a pretty glen. They secured their horses, and Karen and the two boys eagerly followed Gordon Halliday to a huge boulder near the edge of the hill.

"This is it, Dan."

The rancher dropped onto one knee, stirring the dirt in front of the boulder with his fingers. "On this very spot your great-grandfather built that famous campfire—probably the last one he ever built."

Dan bent close, studying intently the side of the rock, darkened by the soot from many fires.

"As I told you," the man went on, "search parties found traces of his last fire, and his abandoned coffee pot. There was no sign of Daniel himself, and no evidence that he had ever gone beyond this point."

"What could have happened to him?" whispered Karen.

"Your guess is as good as mine."

Dan straightened up, saying nothing. He slowly pivoted

about, looking first in one direction and then in another —trying to project himself back into the last century.

What had happened here seventy-three years ago? What force of man or Nature had surprised a lonely gold-seeker at his fire and obliterated all trace of him? Would they ever know the answer?

"What made old Daniel camp way up here, Mr. Halliday?" It was Robert who asked the question. He was now leaning against the boulder beside the ranch foreman, gazing down the hill. "Why didn't he camp down in the canyon, where there is shelter?" he added.

"Probably because of the storm," Mr. Halliday replied. "No wise man of the West ever makes his camp in the canyons during the rainy season."

"That's right, Rob." Karen, who was running a comb through her short dark curls, looked at her cousin. "Didn't you ever hear of flash floods?" she demanded. "A wall of water can rush down that canyon and sweep a man off his feet in a second. It happens lots of times in this country."

Robert stared back at the girl, but he didn't seem to be listening to her. "Dan believes that his great-grandfather was really murdered by Apaches," he said thoughtfully to Mr. Halliday, "but weren't the Apaches on reservations by 1889?"

"Yes," the man agreed, "most of them were. But some had left the tribes already and were living in the valley; and there might have been a lone-wolf Indian up in these hills who had refused to submit. In fact, there is some evidence that this was so. Dan may have told you about Tom Weeder."

"Tom Weeder?" Robert frowned.

"Tom was an old prospector who lived on the mountain. He came into the town of Tombstone leading Daniel

Glover's horse, a few days after the disappearance. Tom swore that he had traded for it with a young Apache he met on the trail. The Indian said that he had found the horse wandering around without a rider."

"Maybe Tom Weeder killed Daniel and stole the horse," said Robert. "He might have tried to get Daniel to tell him where the gold mine was, and when he wouldn't——"

"No, according to the records, Tom was as reliable as the sun. Of course, he was questioned, but the sheriff cleared him completely."

Dan appeared just then. He had been stalking around, getting the lay of the land.

"I still vote for the Apache," he said stubbornly. He pointed to a ledge part of the way up the granite bluff. It was now in deep shadow. "Why couldn't the Indian have crept down to that ledge with a gun—or even with a bow and arrow—while Daniel sat in front of his camp-fire? It would have been simple to put a shot in his back."

"Then what did he do with the body?" demanded Karen.

"He could have buried it."

Gordon Halliday spoke up. "This area was searched pretty carefully by many men, including Daniel's own brother. Naturally, nobody can be sure that your great-grandfather even died on this spot, Dan. And at this late date, I don't think we'll come any closer to solving that mystery. We'd better concentrate on looking for the lost mine and let old Daniel's spirit rest in peace."

He walked toward his horse and began to unload. "How about getting wood for the fire, boys?" he suggested. "It will soon be dark. I'll consult with Karen about what we'll have to eat."

When the boys came up from the canyon a little later,

each with an armload of wood, they dumped it near the big boulder.

"Let's build our fire right here," said Dan, pointing to the spot where, seventy-three years before, his ill-fated ancestor had boiled his coffee.

Later, as they sat around the campfire, while Karen helped prepare their supper of pancakes and bacon, the boys pondered the next day's journey. Robert got his map out and he and Dan studied it by the flickering light of the flames.

"Which direction do we go tomorrow?" Dan asked.

"That's the problem." Gordon Halliday moved close to the boys, squatting for a moment to look over their shoulders. "From here on out, the trail to the lost gold mine is anybody's guess."

He put his finger about halfway across the map. "We must be about here," he stated. "But as you realize by now this map is very roughly drawn. Daniel Glover evidently meant it only as a general guide for his own use. Directions and distances are hard to estimate in such uneven country."

Danny squinted at the faded lettering. "The next place we want to look for is something called the Needle," he said hopefully. "How are we going to find that?"

"I'm not sure. Not far from here, to the north, there's a huge hole in the mountain. You can see the sky through it. . . . Some old-timers in the valley believe that Daniel Glover used that for one of his landmarks and called it the Needle. On the other hand, off to the northeast there is an extensive badlands region, with hundreds of sandstone formations in strange shapes. Daniel's Needle might be among them."

Dan and Robert looked hopelessly at each other. Noticing their long faces, Halliday laughed.

"I warned you that this mine wouldn't be easy to find," he said. "We might be looking for the famous 'needle in the haystack' and *never* find it. I'd suggest that you wait until morning and then climb up onto the bluff and look around the countryside. Then you can decide which trail looks more promising."

He moved back to the other side of the fire, to help poor Karen in her valiant struggles with the pancake batter. As he scraped some of the embers from beneath the frying pan so it wouldn't be so hot, smoke curled around the coffee pot.

Later, when Dan was stretched out near his cousin in his bedroll, he saw the big ranch foreman get up and empty the dregs from his coffee pot over the coals. Once more, smoke rolled up, and some of it curled down in a curious way at the base of the boulder.

Strange wind currents in this canyon, thought Dan sleepily. The coiling smoke reminded him of the little spool of paper he had put away in his box of arrowheads back at the ranch.

He stirred restlessly, feeling that somehow he was missing a clue that might even help them find that needle in the haystack.

The boys were out early in the morning, and after breakfast they sought the easiest access to the top of the decomposed granite bluff and scrambled up the side. Karen begged to join them, but when Dan pointed sternly to the pile of breakfast dishes, she went obediently to wash them.

Both Dan and Robert had secretly admitted to each

other that there were some advantages in having a girl in camp. After all, who likes to do dirty dishes? And Karen had been a good sport about it, so far.

From the top of the bluff, the boys were able to look off for many miles in every direction.

"There's the hole in the mountain!" Dan cried suddenly, pointing to the north. He could see the pale blue of the morning sky through an elongated hole in a rounded dome of rock. "It looks exactly like the eye of a needle."

"Yes, it does," agreed Robert. But meanwhile, he had shaded his eyes and was looking toward the east where, beyond a series of canyons, lay a weird wonderland of rocks. From a pool of morning haze rose fantastic domes and spires.

"It seems more likely to me that Daniel Glover's needle is over there," he said. "It could be one of those tall, pillar-like formations."

"I don't think so," Dan insisted. "The eye in the mountain is more likely to remind a person of a needle than a pillar of rock is."

"Well, in Central Park in New York, there's an obelisk of stone from ancient Egypt called Cleopatra's Needle. Daniel might have been thinking of that."

That did it. "I vote for the needle's eye," Dan said stubbornly. "After all, a real needle has a hole in it."

"I think we're more likely to find Daniel's landmark if we cross over to those badlands," snapped Robert.

The boys were still arguing heatedly as they climbed down the hill. But when they reached the camp and saw that Karen and Mr. Halliday had the camp cleaned and everything ready to go, they were in accord again. It was Robert who gave in.

84)

"We've decided to go up to the needle's eye, Mr. Halliday," he said, to Dan's surprise.

"I hoped you would," said Karen happily, "I brought my camera, and I want you to take a snapshot of me standing right in that opening."

In only a few moments, all four were mounted once more, riding northward along the edge of another of the eternal canyons.

9
Phantoms in the Smoke

Riding along behind his cousin, as usual, Dan noticed again how easy on the horse Robert was. After two days in the mountains he was riding like a veteran. With his plaid shirt open at the neck, his hair tousled by the wind and his cheeks ruddy with sunburn, he seemed little like the somewhat prim and pallid character Dan had first encountered in the rain on the road to the ranch.

The Eastern boy was full of enthusiasm, and uncomplaining, and Dan was more than ever glad that he had become a part of this adventure. The only thing that irked Dan now and then was Robert's superior knowledge. Robert not only was up on science and history but must have read every book in the library about Arizona, thought Dan.

When Dan had carelessly mistaken a cactus wren for

a flicker and the other boy had set him straight, it made Dan feel like a tenderfoot in his own country.

It took only a couple of hours for the party to reach the opening in the mountain. The riders came out finally onto a rocky plateau, and there it was above them—a great uneven hole bored by nature. The sky burned blue behind it.

"We'd better take a look at the map now," suggested Mr. Halliday when they had all dismounted.

"Oh, first let's go up there and look through the hole to the other side!" cried Karen. She was rummaging through her saddlebag and came up with her tiny camera. She put the carrying strap over her shoulder, and before anyone could protest she had started to clamber over the rocky incline.

The boys, just as eager, were right at her heels.

It was an exhausting climb and they were all panting when they reached the hole in the mountain. They found the opening much deeper than they had anticipated, and had to climb over jagged rocks to look through to the valley beyond.

The view was so vast and exhilarating that Dan felt as though he were looking down upon half the world. This must be the way the astronauts feel, he thought.

"I hope Daniel's mine isn't on that side of the eye," Robert said in dismay. "We'd never find it."

"I don't think it is," Dan replied. "The map clearly shows it on the other slope. We'd better get back to the horses," he said.

"Not just yet, Dan." Karen had spied a jutting rock and was climbing up the side of it. She took a precarious position on top of it.

"Get down from there, Karen!" Dan shouted furiously. "Do you want to break your neck?"

But she stood up, silhouetted against the opening. Then she dangled her camera down where Robert could reach it. "Take my picture, Rob," she pleaded. She posed.

Dan held his breath as Robert backed away and took two snapshots. Then Dan himself grabbed the camera and snapped it shut. He ordered the reckless girl down in no uncertain terms.

"Be careful now," he said. But just as he feared, coming down the rock was more hazardous than going up had been. Karen tumbled the last few feet and scraped her leg.

"Ouch!" she said.

White-lipped, Dan bent down to examine the injury. Then he took out a clean handkerchief and wrapped it around his sister's leg to stop the bleeding.

"I should have known better than to bring a peanut-brain like you along," he said. "If you aren't careful you're going to ruin this whole expedition."

"I'm sorry, Dan. I'll be ever so careful——"

Dan turned away and started back through the tunnel, leaving Robert to help the repentent girl down the hill.

Gordon Halliday also took a serious view of Karen's foolish behavior. "You're just fortunate you didn't smash that leg," he told her, as he opened the first-aid kit she had brought along. He painted the wound with medicine and bound it lightly with gauze. Then he spread a blanket over some pine needles and made her lie down for a few minutes.

"Stay right there where I can keep an eye on you," he ordered. "If we have another accident of any kind, we go right back to the Bar-Alpha, gold mine or no gold mine."

While Halliday was tending to Karen's injury, Dan and Robert looked for the hundredth time at the old map. "The next thing to look out for is this Camel Rock," said Robert. "I suppose it's something shaped like a camel. There's an arrow pointing east."

Mr. Halliday now came up beside Dan and they both stared off to the east. They were at a fairly high elevation and the hillsides were heavily wooded.

"No telling how far this Camel Rock might be," Halliday remarked thoughtfully. "But it must be over there somewhere if we're on the right track."

"I don't see a thing that even faintly resembles a camel," Dan said glumly.

"Let's scout around a bit anyway," suggested Robert cheerfully. "It could be just a small rock formation, and the trees might even have hidden it in seventy years."

"Everything from now on is guesswork," put in Mr. Halliday. "All we can do is follow our hunches."

As soon as the subdued Karen felt able to mount her horse again, they struck out across the rocky plateau toward a stand of blue spruce. They rode down one hill and up another; into one densely wooded canyon and out on the other side—only to be confronted by more canyons.

There were few rock formations in the area and the earth beneath the horses' hooves was carpeted with leaf-mold. For a long time, the only glimpse of sky they had was through the tops of pine and fir.

Mr. Halliday, on unfamiliar ground now, blazed their trail and checked his compass several times.

Toward noon, Dan brought his plodding little range horse to an abrupt halt. He called the others to come back. Their canteens, last filled at Coffee Pot Hill, were almost empty, and they had found no fresh spring. Dan was beginning to get discouraged and anxious and Karen's close call had unnerved him.

"I guess I was wrong," he admitted, as the others rode up. "This is a wild goose chase and it's all my fault. . . . What shall we do now, Mr. Halliday?"

"Well, I don't know, Dan. It might be best to go back to our last campground at Coffee Pot Hill and spend the night there. It's a little early, but Karen can get a good rest, and we can start our search again early in the morning."

"Or maybe we should go up again and see if that camel went through the needle's eye," said Robert with a laugh.

Dan took the teasing with good grace. He was disgusted with himself. A whole day was shot because of his stubbornness. He could see now that it would have been wiser to strike out for the badlands in search of the Needle.

Mr. Halliday, seeing his distress, put a hand lightly on Dan's shoulder. "You're not the first gold seeker to become confused by Daniel Glover's crazy map," he stated. "Prospectors have been wild-goose-chasing over these hills for over seventy years. I think we can be allowed one lost day."

"Besides, you could still be right," Robert added generously. "But since we've drawn a blank in this direction, how about heading back to Coffee Pot Hill? We can test my theory tomorrow, and—what's that?"

A weird and totally unexpected sound had vibrated on the air—the loud and raucous bray of a donkey. It was not far distant.

Riding toward the sound, they soon came to a small clearing. To their surprise, they encountered two men relaxing under a tree. Nearby was tethered a restless donkey, loaded with camping equipment and miners' tools.

"Well, Judd Mason!" Mr. Halliday got down from his horse and strode toward the men, holding out his hand. "Are you still looking for lost gold mines, too?" he asked.

The two men rose and the shorter of the two—one with grizzled gray hair and bright blue eyes—shook hands warmly with the Bar-Alpha foreman. "Yep," he said. "I've been searching these canyons for old Daniel Glover's mine for ten years and I don't intend to give up till I've found that gold. . . . This is Frank Carlos, Halliday."

He indicated the man at his side, and Frank Carlos held out his own hand, smiling.

"In the winter, Frank's one of the crack lawyers in my company down in Phoenix," explained Judd Mason. "But I talked him into prospecting Mystery Mountain with me this summer. He's the best Indian guide on or off of the Reservation, and if anybody can find old Daniel's mine, Frank can."

Dan took a second look at the stranger. He was a handsome young man, with black hair and strong bronzed features. He *was* an Indian, Dan saw, and from the looks of him, he could easily be a true Apache.

Mr. Halliday turned and introduced Karen and the two boys, who were now dismounted and standing behind him, to the two men.

"I told you there would be competition for your mine, Rob and Dan," he remarked with a laugh. "These two boys are the great-grandsons of the original owners of the Phantom Pony, Judd," he said. "They think it should by rights belong to them, and they're searching for it right now."

92)

The two men shook hands with the boys. The quiet, black-haired one tipped his hat politely to Karen. Then, for the first time, he spoke.

"And I think the Phantom Pony should belong to me," he said, with a pleasant grin. "After all, my great-grand-fathers lived in these hills before the white man ever set eyes on them. This was all Apache land." He waved his hand in a wide arc.

"That's sure true!" Dan said impulsively. He had that vague feeling of shame that many Americans feel when they remember how unjustly the Indians were sometimes treated in the Old West. "The white man wasn't always fair to the Indians."

The big man laughed. "And the Indian wasn't always fair to the white men," he admitted. "He sometimes ran off with their scalps! But that's past history now, young man. We are both Americans, you and I."

While the man talked, Judd Mason had taken a piece of folded paper from his pocket and was opening it. Danny saw with surprise that it was a copy of the same map he had found in the old chest!

"I've spent the past five summers over in that section," Mr. Mason said. He had squatted down with the map in front of him while the others stood around looking at it. He pointed to the right side of the paper. "I've checked every crazy sandstone formation in the Badlands," he admitted, "and I ended up by going in circles."

He looked up toward the hole in the mountain. "Now, Frank here has a theory that we'll find a clue of some kind up there around the hole in the rocks, so we're trying that next."

"That's right." The Indian pointed to the north. "There

were many legends about this lost mine among the Apaches. When I was a small boy on the Reservation the old braves used to sit around and talk about Daniel Glover. They called him the Man with Wings on His Face, because of his big mustache.

"They said he used to sit up there in the opening of the rocks—shouting in some crazy language."

"Probably spouting Greek poetry," put in Robert with a laugh.

"Perhaps. Anyway, I think it possible that he scratched some clue on the rocks up there. It might point the way to the mine."

"As far as we know," said Mr. Mason, getting to his feet and folding his map, "Daniel himself might still be up around there. I've always felt that if I could locate the old fellow's remains I'd find the lost mine."

He turned, then, to the boys. "As a matter of fact," he said, "we're on our way up there now. Do you want to join our company?"

"I guess not," Dan said uncertainly. He glanced toward Robert. "We just got through scouting around up there. We decided there was more chance over in the Badlands region."

Judd Mason laughed. He picked up his hat, which had fallen, and jammed it on his gray head. "Well, watch out for mountain lions," he warned. "I won't wish you luck, because if you find the mine first, I'm out of luck."

Frank Carlos shook hands all around. "As a lawyer, I can tell you that the Phantom Pony Mine will belong to the first party that locates the ore and stakes a legal claim to it. You have as much chance as anyone."

He stood waving as the three young people and Halliday rode off down the trail.

"I don't understand why your Aunt Charlotte let everybody and his uncle get hold of that map, Dan," Robert remarked in some disgust. "It should have been kept secret."

"I suppose it couldn't be," Dan answered, from his side. "When Daniel disappeared, his family was so anxious to find him that they didn't think about the gold. They gave the search parties copies of the map in hopes that it would help them follow his trail."

Meeting the two prospectors had been pleasant enough, Dan thought, but it was discouraging to know that Mason had searched for years and found no trace of the mine. What chance did Dan and Robert have, with only a few days to spend on the mountain?

In some spooky way, Robert seemed to read Dan's thoughts. Anyway, his next remark was a direct answer to them.

"We still have something Mason doesn't have, Dan," he said. "My copy of the map has those Greek symbols on it. They haven't helped us yet, but I have a hunch they are really important."

The return trip was quick and uneventful, for much of it was downhill. The first thing that the two boys did when they arrived at Coffee Pot Hill was to lead their thirsty horses down to the stream. And though both boys considerately offered to water Karen's mount, the girl determinedly limped after them and tended to him herself. She had been unusually quiet and angelic since her fall.

"Right back where we started from," Dan Glover muttered morosely. Maybe we would have been wiser to have

gone back to the rock with Mr. Mason, he was thinking.

He was still moody when he crawled into his bedroll before the smouldering fire that night.

Through half-closed eyes he watched the smoke rising like phantoms from the fire. There was something strange about the way that smoke behaved. . . . Instead of drifting up into the atmosphere, it curled down against the boulder. Down, down . . . down. Why?

Dan drifted off into a troubled sleep.

10 / Dark Discovery

Dan must have slept soundly, for when he awoke, Gordon Halliday was already up and once more busy building a fire, to prepare breakfast. The smoke billowed up—and down.

Dan sat up with a reflexive jerk, for now he knew what had troubled him: the smoke was being sucked under the rock!

He zipped open his sleeping bag and hauled on his boots. Then, without a word to the startled Halliday, he ran around the big boulder and halfway down the hill.

There, faintly, faintly, on the morning air, he saw a tiny wisp of white smoke coming out of the ground. It was seeping from beneath another boulder on the hillside.

Dan stared at the spot for a long moment. There was a cave inside that hill. A hidden cave!

"What's eating you, Dan?"

Gordon Halliday had appeared at the top of the hill. He was followed by Robert and Karen, both blinking sleepily and tugging on their jackets.

"I've found a cave in the hill!" Dan shouted up to them.

"What's so exciting about that?" Robert demanded. He came, half stumbling, to stand beside his cousin. "There must be lots of caves in these mountains."

"Sure," agreed Dan, "but there's something mighty funny about this one." He pointed to the rock he had discovered, and then to a depression beside it on the ground. "That rock must be wedged over the opening of a cave. See—it looks as though it had been moved from over there."

He explained how he had discovered the hollow under the ground by watching the curious action of the smoke from the campfire.

Mr. Halliday and Karen were standing beside the boulder now. The man frowned as he kicked with the toe of his boot around the base of the rock.

"I believe you're right, Dan," he said. "Smoke is being drawn under that big boulder above and is seeping out right here. There is at least a passageway under here. And this rock has been shifted—probably years ago. But I still don't understand why you're so excited——"

"Don't you see, sir?" Dan interrupted him. "If somebody did happen to hide in a cave under here, and was followed by a—a pursuer, and then was found, well, maybe whoever was after him tipped this rock over the entrance to the cave and imprisoned him!"

"Daniel Glover, you mean? Is that what you are suggesting, Dan?" Mr. Halliday's eyes were contemplative.

"Well, why not?" Dan said stubbornly.

"But wouldn't the search parties have discovered that this rock had been recently moved?" protested Robert. "You can still see where it originally sat."

"Not necessarily," Dan insisted. "Not if it had been an Indian who shoved that rock over. He could have camouflaged this spot with dirt and brush, so you'd never even suspect a cave was under here. The searchers probably passed right by, and if somebody was in there, he was probably dead and couldn't call out——"

By now, Robert was looking at his Arizona cousin with frank admiration. "Boy, you've got some imagination, Dan!" he declared. Then he frowned. "But how are we going to test your theory?"

He bent over the rock, heaving at it mightily. It didn't budge.

"I don't know," Dan said in despair. "That rock's so well settled by now, we'll never be able to shove it out of the way. And we don't have tools to dig it out. This whole hill is made of decomposed granite." He was scraping hopelessly around the boulder with a sharp stone.

"I've got an idea," cried Robert suddenly. "We'll use a lever. . . . Remember what old Archimedes said?" he added with a laugh. "'Give me a place to stand and I will move the world.'"

"Of course!" Dan cried, jumping up. "Why didn't 1 think of that?"

Gordon Halliday smiled at the two boys who were so much alike. "Well, we'll leave the problem in your hands," he said. "You two figure out how to move the world while Karen and I go back and stir up some breakfast. We want to get an early start today on our trail to the pot of gold. Come on, Karen."

Karen looked as though she much preferred to stay and supervise the project on the hillside, but she had been on her best behavior since her accident of the previous day. She followed Mr. Halliday meekly back to camp.

The boys wasted no time in getting down to the stream bed in search of a piece of driftwood that could be used as a lever. They found a stout pole about eleven feet long which they dragged triumphantly up the hill.

With the camp hatchet they cleaned it up and soon had one end of it wedged beneath the side of the boulder. Dan found a small rock for a fulcrum.

At first, they were unable to budge the big rock; it was too well settled; but by moving their fulcrum about and wedging tree limbs beneath it, they soon got the boulder bouncing. Suddenly it lost balance and went crashing down into the canyon, leaving a gaping hole uncovered on the hillside.

"It is a cave!" cried Robert. "You were right."

The two boys made a rush for the entrance. They were soon on their knees, heads almost touching, peering into the dark recess below. The smell of smoke from the campfire was strong now, but at first they could see nothing at all. In their very eagerness to see, they blocked out the light.

Then Dan lowered his head into the hole and looked around carefully. On the floor of the cave, off to one side, he saw something that glittered.

"Go bring a flashlight, Rob," he begged, his voice tense with excitement. "I think there's gold down there!"

Robert obediently jumped to his feet and ran back up

the hill. He returned in a moment, accompanied by Gordon Halliday and Dan's sister. He knelt down and shoved the flashlight into his cousin's waiting hand.

"Hurry up and tell us what you see," Rob begged. "Is there really gold down there?"

Dan snapped on the flashlight and turned it in the direction of the faint gleam. Then he gasped. "It's gold, all right." His voice came back muffled. "It's a great big old gold watch and chain!"

"Do you see anything else, Dan?" demanded Karen.

Dan slowly swept the torch around the sides of the rocky cave. Then his heart went into a measured, thudding beat that shook his entire being.

A few feet from the huge watch lay a shoe—a man's old-fashioned leather shoe. It was shriveled and twisted by time.

11

Daniel's Last Ride

Dan Glover lifted his dark head once more into the sunshine and backed away from the cave opening. He was pale around the lips, and when he met the questioning looks of the others, he glanced away.

"What's the matter, Dan?" Karen was pale, too, and her blue eyes were wide.

"Old Daniel m—must have been down there all right," Dan said. "There's a man's shoe in there. It's all dried up."

Nothing much was said while Robert and Mr. Halliday took turns with the flashlight, inspecting the dark cavern in the hillside. Even Karen crept gingerly to the edge of the hole and peered inside. Then for a while they all stood around the opening, discussing their sobering discovery.

"It must have happened just about as Dan thought,"

remarked Robert. "Mr. Glover knew he was going to be ambushed and ran into this canyon. Then he saw the entrance to the cave and decided he could hide in there——"

"And whoever was trying to get him followed his trail and tipped the big rock over the entrance," said Dan. "It was probably balanced right there"—he pointed to the depression—"so that a good shove was all that was needed."

"But what happened then?" Robert was frowning. "And why did he take off his shoe? Do you think"—the boy hesitated before voicing the question that was in all their minds—"do you think he's still down there somewhere? I noticed a narrow passageway on one side. It looked as though it might lead farther into the hill."

Halliday nodded. "That could be, Rob. Some of the caves in this country are very extensive. There could even be another entrance to this one."

"If there is"—Karen just whispered the words—"Daniel Glover might have escaped!"

"Who knows?" Then Mr. Halliday smiled. "Wait a minute, kids, we're forgetting one thing. We aren't even sure that Great-grandad Glover was even down there."

"Well, there's one way to find out."

Dan straightened up and looked at the man. "I'll go down there and get that big watch, Mr. Halliday. I'd like to take it back to Aunt Charlotte at the ranch. She'll know soon enough if it belonged to her father."

Mr. Halliday hesitated for a moment. "All right, Dan," he said finally. "Just take the watch, though, and don't disturb anything else. There may have been a crime committed here, and even if it did happen seventy-three years ago, the sheriff's office would want to investigate before anything is touched."

So, feet first, Dan slipped through the opening in the hill, and dropped lightly to the floor of the cave. His heartbeat was like a tom-tom as he turned and reached back for the flashlight.

"Watch out for snakes," cautioned his cousin, from above.

Dan looked warily around. Smoke was still drifting down into the cave from a crack under the rock near their campfire. It floated through the beam of light that he played over the rocky walls.

The narrow passageway Robert had mentioned twisted off into the darkness at one side. Danny wondered with a heavy heart what lay beyond that opening, but he didn't investigate. He moved with bent head, stooping to pick up the watch. It felt smooth and heavy in his hand and he slipped it into his pocket. Then he wasted no time getting out of the murky cavern.

"Why, it isn't even dulled," Dan declared, as he pulled it out and showed it to his companions. He turned it over in his hands and it gleamed golden in the morning sunlight. The back was decorated with intricate engraving.

"That looks like a monogram," remarked Robert. He took the watch from his cousin, to study it closely. Then he whistled softly. "It belonged to Daniel Glover all right! Look at those initials—D-E-G."

His serious brown eyes met Dan's.

Robert pressed gently on the stem of the old watch. It stuck at first, then sprang open, revealing a fancy enameled face with Roman numerals. The watch had stopped at three minutes of twelve.

"What do we do next?"

Gordon Halliday asked the question as they sat eating their belated breakfast. "Do you partners intend to go on with the search for the gold mine, or do you think that we should head back to the Bar-Alpha and report this discovery to the authorities?"

Dan looked up from his hot cakes in some consternation. He had been so excited about finding the cave that he had temporarily lost sight of their main objective. "What do you say, Robert?"

"I hate to give up looking for the mine," Robert said slowly, "but we probably should go back. Now that the cave is open, somebody might find it and mess up the evidence before the sheriff can make his search."

"And anyway," Karen had her say, "Aunt Charlotte would want to know right away what we found."

With some reluctance, Dan agreed. While Mr. Halliday and Karen broke camp, the two boys did their best to disguise the opening of the cave with tree limbs. They were not too happy about leaving it unexplored.

There were still many unanswered questions about Daniel Glover. Why had he taken off one shoe and left it down there? Where had he gone? Were there other relics of the lost miner in the depths of that hill? Was there even, perhaps, a clue to the location of the very thing they longed to find—the Phantom Pony Mine?

"I just hope that Mr. Judd Mason and that Indian guide of his don't come snooping around here in the next few days," Dan said to Robert. He had just re-membered Mason's theory—that if he could find Daniel Glover's remains, he could break the riddle of the location of the lost mine.

The two-day trip back to the Bar-Alpha ranch lacked excitement, for the trial was familiar now, and the party pushed along steadily, anxious to reach the ranch with the news of their weird discovery.

Early in the afternoon of the second day they came down out of the hills within sight of the Bar-Alpha ranch. Karen, now fully recovered from her slight accident, spied Chapo on the trail ahead. The Mexican cowhand was astride Dan's pet, Chili.

With a shout of pleasure at the sight of an old friend, Karen pushed her horse past Mr. Halliday and galloped ahead to meet the cowboy. Robert and Dan, following her lead, took out after her, raising a cloud of dust in the warm summer air.

They all slowed as they came near, and Chapo waited to greet them, leaning forward in Chili's saddle. His brown face crinkled with pleasure at seeing them, but there was surprise in his eyes, too.

"Why you come back so soon?" Chapo asked, when the youthful trio had gathered around him. The horses were bobbing their heads up and down in their own peculiar style of greeting. "You find the gold mine, yes?" he de-manded, his eyes twinkling.

Dan laughed ruefully. "We find the gold mine, *no*," he answered. His face shadowed. "But we did make a dis-covery, Chapo," he added. "That's why we cut our search for the mine short. We think we found a clue to what happened to Aunt Charlotte's father. We want to tell her."

The old man nodded and slowly turned his horse around. "She is waiting for you," he said. "She see you coming up on the trail. She send me to meet you."

By this time Gordon Halliday had joined them, and the five rode in silence to the ranch.

"Yes, that must be my father's watch."

Charlotte Glover sat in her wheelchair, examining the watch that Dan had handed to her. "Those were his initials," she said. "D.E.G.—Daniel Eversham Glover."

The old woman had listened with little display of emotion to Dan's story of the strange discovery at Coffee Pot Hill, but now he noticed that her frail fingers trembled as she touched the engraving on the back of the gold watch case.

She faced the ranch foreman, who was standing in the doorway of the living room. "I take it, Gordon, that you believe that my father died in that cave," she said.

Halliday nodded gravely. "Yes, I do, Miss Charlotte."

"Well, it all happened a long time ago." Aunt Charlotte looked around at the anxious faces of Karen and the two boys. "Just remember this," she said gently, "my father would have been dead now in any event. . . . Still, if his bones are found up there, I'd like to have them brought down from the mountain."

"That's already been arranged for." Gordon Halliday walked over to the couch and settled his long frame against the cushions. "I telephoned Tom Ligget, the county sheriff, as soon as I got in, and reported our discovery. He thinks, as I do, that Daniel Glover must have crawled deeper into those caverns and was trapped there —unless there is another exit, of course.

"Tom has asked me to go back to the mountain with him in the morning to point out the cave. If your father's remains are found, a lot of riddles may be solved."

"You mean you are going to ride right back up there again, Mr. Halliday?" demanded Karen. "I should think you'd be worn out from riding so much. I know I am."

The foreman smiled. "I feel more easy in a saddle than I do in a rocking chair, Karen," he said. "But we're not taking the horses this trip. To save time, the county charters a helicopter for such operations as this. We can fly in and out of those hills in a jiffy."

"Can we go along?" In twin voices Dan and Robert shouted their plea.

To their disappointment, Mr. Halliday shook his head. "We will be crowded as it is, boys. Besides the pilot and the sheriff, we may have some deputies with us."

On the following morning, from an upstairs window in Old House, Karen and the two boys watched the mosquitolike contraption, with its spinning propeller, sail up over Signal Point and disappear in the vastness of the rugged range.

A few hours later, it came whirring noisily back over the valley and dropped down in front of the ranch house. Gordon Halliday climbed out.

Dan had already wheeled Aunt Charlotte's chair out onto the porch and Mr. Ligget, the sheriff, got out of the plane and came up to speak to her.

He took off his wide-brimmed hat. "We brought the remains of your father down from the mountain, Miss Glover," he said respectfully. "We found a number of his

personal effects in the cave also. We will turn those over to you when our investigation is completed.

"Just as we suspected, Daniel had crawled deeper into the caverns, searching, I suppose, for an exit, and was finally trapped. Gordon will want to tell you about it."

12

Diary of the Dead

After the plane had taken off again, Gordon Halliday sat on the step, surrounded by the ranch family, including Chapo and Chavela. Quietly he told about the latest findings on the mountain.

"In some uncanny way, Dan guessed right all along," he said, looking thoughtfully at the boy. "His great-grandfather was shot by an Indian called Coyote Joe."

"How you know that, Mr. Halliday?" Chapo asked, his black eyes agleam with interest.

"Well, Daniel Glover left a strange diary during the last days of his life—very crudely written, of course, because of the terrible conditions. The first entries were written on the trail, when he was afraid of being ambushed. Later, after he had been trapped in the cave, he had to scribble his thoughts down in total darkness."

Mr. Halliday drew a small notebook from his pocket.

"Daniel wrote this on the backs of old letters. They were preserved only because he put them in his leather wallet and wedged the wallet into a niche in the cave. The edges were chewed slightly by rodents, but the diary is quite readable.

"Tom Ligget took the original with him, of course," the foreman went on, "but he let me copy it first. Listen. . . ."

The others sat spellbound as Halliday read aloud the moving words that Daniel Glover had scratched in pencil so many years before.

"*August 3rd, 1889.* Followed trail to the mine—making notes for brother James. That crazy Indian—Coyote Joe—watching my every move from the cliff. I do not trust him.

"*August 4th*—Ambushed while cooking breakfast. Shot through the foot by same Indian. He ran off with my horse. Must try to lie low till this foot improves . . . Later—Hiding in a cave in hill—hope he doesn't trail me here. Still have pistol.

"*August 5th—or 6th*—Foot too swollen for shoe. I will try to get out. Too late—Indian came in night and blocked entrance to cave. Now in total darkness. If I don't find other exit I am doomed. I wonder what— what time it is. Lost my watch—too dark to see it anyway. Love to my dear wife and children—God bless them"

Mr. Halliday looked up. There was a heavy silence. "That's the end," he said finally. "But it tells a lot, and clears up the mystery of Daniel's disappearance."

"But it doesn't tell us anything about where the mine

is located," Danny said at last. He wouldn't have been a boy and human if he hadn't felt deeply disappointed. "Weren't there any other papers in that wallet?"

"There were some assay reports on the mine, some clippings." The man shrugged. "There were other things, of course. A pistol, a penknife—some coins, I think. The sheriff's deputy wrapped them up and put them in the plane, but I didn't pay much attention. I was too busy copying Daniel's diary."

The discovery of the skeleton on the mountain created quite a sensation in the Southwest. The old legends of lost mines and Apache raids were dug out of the files and printed in all the papers. Reporters from newspapers and television studios came out to the ranch to interview Danny and to marvel at how he had discovered the hidden cave by watching smoke from the campfire.

After the authorities had made their investigation and the coroner's office had reported its findings, the remains of Daniel Glover were properly interred in the cemetery where Aunt Charlotte's mother lay buried.

A simple service was held, and out of respect for Charlotte Glover, Dan's parents came out from the city, and the neighboring ranchers attended. It was a solemn affair, but not a sad one, for no one present had known the dead man except Aunt Charlotte herself, and she scarcely remembered him.

Danny and Robert felt somewhat let down after all the excitement was over. They had gone through a great deal, the summer was ending, and they were still no closer to taking possession of the Phantom Pony Mine than they had ever been.

"It's too late to go back on the mountain this year," Danny told Robert gloomily that night after the memorial service, as they went up to their room. "Your mother will be coming back from California before long, to take you back to Boston. And I'll soon have to leave the Bar-Alpha and go back to school." He groaned aloud at the mere thought.

"Well, maybe I can come to Arizona next summer and we can look for the mine again," Robert remarked, as he took off his suit coat and hung it in the closet. But his expression was as gloomy as Robert's.

"I just don't feel so sure we're going to find it anyway," he added. "That's an awfully big mountain, and old Daniel's crazy map isn't going to help much, I'm afraid."

"I'm going to keep searching for that mine, just the same," Dan said stubbornly. "Who knows, maybe we'll still find the key to the map." He didn't want to give up the dream of a lifetime, yet he could think of nothing more hopeful to say.

"Let's forget it for now, and have a game of chess before we hit the sack," he suggested.

He looked around for the chessboard, and then remembered that it was in Karen's room, so he walked down the hall and tapped on his sister's door.

"Come in," she called.

Dan opened the door. His sister was in her robe and slippers, standing before the mirror. Her pretty face was twisted slightly, as she busied herself in the manner of young females everywhere with the complicated process of putting her hair up for the night.

Dan saw the chessboard on the table near her bed and went to pick it up. The chessmen were out of the box and

(117

he began to put them back. As he did so, he glanced up at Karen, grinning critically.

"You look like a woman from Mars adjusting her antenna," he declared.

Karen glared at him. She picked up a strand of hair and wound it around and around a pink plastic roller. "Get out!" she retorted.

But Dan couldn't move. *Roller-scroller.* The silly phrase had simply popped into his mind, and then his brain began to click like a magic computer. Like a problem in math, the puzzle added up.

Hair curler; curler-roller; roller-scroll; cipher-cane!

"I've got it!" he shouted wildly.

The box of chessmen flew from his hands, and they scattered in every direction. Before Karen could turn around, he had dashed from the room and was on his way to tell Robert. In another instant, curlers and all, she was on his heels.

Robert, who was just taking off his tie, looked up in surprise when Dan burst into the room.

"Where's that cane you used when you hurt your ankle?" Dan asked. His eyes searched the room. Spying the gold-headed cane in the corner, he ran and took it up.

While his cousin and sister watched him in complete bafflement, he got the tiny scroll of paper out of its receptacle in the cane. Then Dan did a curious thing. He sat down on the edge of the bed and began very carefully to wind the long strip of yellowed paper around the top part of Daniel Glover's cane just below the gold knob.

He studied it, frowning, and then unwound it and began all over again. Then, triumphantly, anchoring the

118)

coiled paper with his thumb, he held the wrapped shaft in front of Robert's eyes.

Robert gasped. The lines of the broken letters had come magically together. Written halfway down the length of the cane were several rows of words, printed in aged brown ink.

"How did you ever figure that out?"

"It's a clever trick the ancient Greeks used to send secret messages in battle," Dan said, smiling. "I read about it the other day in that book we found in the old chest—*Plutarch's Lives*. But I didn't see the connection here until I watched Karen rolling up her hair."

Meanwhile, Karen herself was bending over the writing with a puzzled look on her face. "But what does it say?" she asked. "It's written in such funny letters—it's just Greek to me!"

For the first time Dan really looked at the words. He recognized several of the letters that were on the map Robert had brought from Boston.

"It *is* Greek," he said in disgust. He turned to his cousin. "I guess you'll have to read it for us, Robert."

It was the other boy's turn to look dismayed. "Me read it? You must think I'm a brain or something! I can't read ancient Greek. I just know a few symbols used in science."

Dan's heart sank. "I feel sure it will tell us something about the Phantom Pony Mine," he said. "But who can read Greek?"

"I know where we can find someone," declared Karen, "but we'll have to take a trip to Tucson!"

13

Thanks to Mr. Plutarch

"I don't understand all the fuss about getting that scrap of paper translated right away."

Aunt Charlotte looked mischievously through her glasses at Karen and the two boys, who had come stampeding down the stairway with a wild request to go to town first thing in the morning. "You can't make another expedition into Mystery Mountain till next year anyway," she told the boys, knowing very well that they were crazy with curiosity. Karen had cleverly suggested that they take their strange document to the Greek department at the university to have it read.

"Please, Aunt Charlotte," the girl pleaded now. "Chapo can take us in the Jeep if Mr. Halliday doesn't have time. And Daddy will know somebody at the U. who can help us."

Her aunt laughed tolerantly. "All right," she said. "Tell Chapo to come here. I must admit I'm a mite curious about that paper myself. The Glover twins would be surprised at all the bother they've caused, with their mysterious maps and secret messages hidden in canes."

The next morning, as they headed for Tucson, Chapo Robles was in his glory, driving the Jeep over the fast modern highway.

Danny, sitting beside him, and Karen and Robert in the back seat joined him in singing the Mexican song, both gay and pathetic, that told of the poor little cricket who couldn't walk.

"La cucaracha, la cucaracha—ya no puede caminar . . ."

Dan felt lighter of heart than he had since that awful moment when he encountered Daniel Glover's old shoe in the cavern on the mountain. Perhaps it was good that they had been forced to give up their first search for the Phantom Pony, he thought. He was sure now that they would never have found it, but perhaps this new clue would lead them to the mine when they took up the search again.

The first thing Chapo did when they reached the city was to drive the young people to Professor Glover's house, near the university.

Dan's parents were greatly surprised, for they had seen their daughter and son only the day before, when they had attended the memorial service, and both Dan and Karen had begged to remain on the ranch for another week.

When Mr. Glover was shown the gold-headed cane, he recognized it at once. "My brothers and I used to stomp around the attic with this when we were kids and visited

Aunt Charlotte," he exclaimed. "But we didn't find this paper in it."

Dan had secured the strip of paper on the cane with transparent tape. "How did you ever figure out the secret of it?" his father asked.

Karen laughed. "Danny actually read a 'dumb old book' this summer, Daddy. He found out there about this way of sending messages."

"It was *Plutarch's Lives*," Robert added. "I read it, too, but didn't stumble onto the trick. It took Dan's clever imagination to see the connection."

Mr. Glover looked pleased, but he wisely made no comment. "Dr. Binns, of the Greek department, lives just down the street," he said. "Let's see what he makes of all this."

Tall, gray-haired Dr. Binns chuckled with delight when Danny handed him the cane with its strange writing and told him of their problem. The professor had finished his summer lectures and was in his garden, puttering around the chrysanthemums.

"It's a kind of scroll," he said instantly. "The *ephors,* the old judges of Sparta, communicated with such a device as this. They had two identical round pieces of wood—called 'em *scytales*. They'd keep one and give one to a general or admiral. The method was better than a cryptogram, because a message written in this way could be read only by using the same device, or its twin."

While the old scholar went to his study to work over the message, his housekeeper served his visitors punch and cookies in the garden, but they were in such suspense that they could scarcely taste the treats.

"A strange document," said Dr. Binns when he came

out at last, with a paper in his hands. "Of course one can't make a literal translation of Greek, but I did my best in the limited time. It seems to be something about a gold mine and a horse's ghost," he said in a puzzled way.

Dan took the paper and in a tense voice read it aloud.

"Promised key to map to gold mine not received—search in vain for horse's ghost. Still have hopes you are alive and God will help aid in solving this dreadful mystery."

Dan looked up to find his own disappointment mirrored in Robert's brown eyes.

"This cane must have belonged to your great-grandfather, Daniel's brother, James," he said at last. "He left it at the ranch, hoping Daniel would return. It doesn't help us at all."

"But where, then, is the other cane?" Karen asked. "Both brothers had canes just alike in that picture Aunt Charlotte has."

"It was probably lost," her father said thoughtfully. "In seventy-three years, it wouldn't be surprising."

It was a deflated trio who returned to the Bar-Alpha that afternoon. They had been right about one thing, they now knew: Daniel Glover had promised his brother a key to the map he had sent to Boston. But if that key had even been recorded, it had never been found. Without it, they could search forever for the Phantom Pony Mine and probably never find it.

"There's a car in the driveway," Karen exclaimed, as

Chapo drove the jeep up the hill and turned it into the lane that led to the ranch house.

It was an official car, and the sheriff got out as they came up behind it. He had a long package in his hands.

"Hello, boys—Karen," he greeted them, as they joined him and walked up the steps. "I came to bring your Aunt Charlotte the few things we found with your grandfather's bones. Our investigation is over and we're through with them."

Dan left Mr. Ligget greeting his aunt in the living room. With murmured excuses he and Robert started to their room, but they were only halfway up the stairs when a shrill cry from Karen brought them dashing down again.

"Danny—Robert," she screamed. "Here it is!"

Mr. Ligget had opened his package on the library table. From across the room Dan could see something gleaming. Along with the pistol, the pocket knife, the buttons and coins, was the gold-headed cane that had belonged to Daniel Glover!

"We can't understand it," Sheriff Ligget was saying. "Why would a man on horseback, who wasn't lame, take a fancy cane like that up into the mountains? And the craziest thing is what we found inside it."

He unscrewed the knob and turned the cane upside down. Out fell two small spools of rolled-up paper!

"They've got some scribbles along the edge of them," he said, frowning. "But none of us at the office could make any sense out of them. Do you suppose, Miss Charlotte, that this has anything to do with that lost mine he was supposed to have up there?"

14

Aunt Charlotte's Whirlygig

"The reason Daniel Glover took the cane with him on that last trip to the mine," said Dan, "was to make these scrolls. Remember, he said in his diary that he'd been making notes for James."

He picked up the cane and showed Mr. Ligget how the strip of paper fitted around it so that the broken letters came together.

"Well, I'll be hanged!" said the sheriff—adding the obvious remark, "It's sure Greek to me."

The others laughed. "The Glover twins seem to have found some use for one of the dead languages," said Aunt Charlotte. "I suppose they started this cane business as a lark when they were students in England, and when Papa made a rich gold strike, they took it up again, and sent these scraps of paper back and forth with secret messages. There were still people in the West who would have killed for gold in those days," she added.

Karen, like the boys, could hardly contain her eagerness. "The question now is, when can we take these things back to Dr. Binns to be translated?" she said.

The old lady pretended dismay, but she was obviously as curious as the rest of them. "As fast as Chapo can get you there, I suppose," she said with a laugh.

This time there was no doubt about it. When Dr. Binns handed Danny his interpretation of the messages on the two small spools of yellowed paper, the boy knew that they had the long-lost key to Daniel Glover's map. For each Greek letter symbol on the map Robert had brought from Boston, there was a corresponding symbol on the scrolls, with explicit instructions for following the trail to the mine.

Danny and his cousin felt sure now that they could go right up on Mystery Mountain and claim their treasure. The only question was *when*. How could they bear to wait for another summer?

Besides the agony of suspense, there was—after all the publicity about the finding of the skeleton—the very real possibility that some other modern prospector or treasure hunter would accidentally stumble on the mine and claim it before they could get there.

To make matters even more difficult, they returned to the ranch to find Robert's mother there, ready to go home to Boston. The first thing she did after greeting her son was to tell him to get his suitcase packed.

"We'll be leaving early in the morning," she said. "I want to get you home and ready to enter school."

It was a pair of gloomy lads who walked up the stairs of the ranch house to the room they had shared for the past weeks.

While Robert folded his clothes, Dan carefully divided his arrowhead collection and put half of the points in a box for his cousin. Then, on impulse, he added his favorite bolo tie.

He had become deeply fond of the other boy, and not only because they were partners in their adventure on the mountain. If Daniel and James Glover had been real twins, Dan and Robert were twins in spirit. For two whole weeks they had lived, laughed, fought, worked and played together. They had shared the biggest adventure of their lives, and the biggest dream. They had become friends.

Now, just when the big dream could come true, the summer was ending and Robert was leaving.

It was Robert himself who expressed their mutual wish aloud, at the dinner table that night. He knew it was hopeless, of course.

"I wish I could stay in Arizona another week, Mother." He looked across the table. "We know we could ride up there and go right to the mine——"

Cousin Marion began to shake her head.

"Well, why don't you?" said Aunt Charlotte.

All eyes turned to stare at the white-haired old lady. If a meteorite had fallen in the middle of the table, they couldn't have been more surprised.

"Why don't we hire one of those whirligig things same as the sheriff did, and you and Dan can fly up there and back in a couple of days.

"What do you think, Gordon?" She addressed the ranch

foreman. "If Marion will wait over for two days, do you think you could arrange it? I'll pay the cost. After all, I've got extra money just sitting in the bank. Of course," she added, with an impish grin, "I'll expect to be paid back with interest, when Dan and Robert get their mine in operation."

"I don't see why it can't be worked out," Mr. Halliday said with enthusiasm. He smiled at the jubilant young partners. "I'll call Tom right after supper and find out how to go about chartering the helicopter."

Dan was still looking in wonder at his amazing old aunt. All the bright ideas in this modern world didn't come from young people, he was thinking.

Then Karen, who had been silent through this discussion, piped up boldly: "When do we go?"

Dan turned to glare at her. He was about to give her an argument, but when he saw the trust in her happy little face, he relented. All right, he thought, let her tag along again. It had been convenient to have somebody to help with the cooking. But she'd better toe the mark! They'd be pushing hard on this last venture; fighting against time to reach the Phantom Pony . . . There'd be no pampering on this trip, even for a girl.

Not very many hours later, the "whirligig" had settled down at the Bar-Alpha like an awkward duckling, to take on the ranch foreman and his three companions. Cousin Marion had generously agreed to delay her return to Boston for two more days, and Robert, Dan and Karen had thrown their belongings together in record time.

And then they were flying over Mystery Moutain. It looked much different from the air, with its rocky crags

glowing pink, gold and lavender in the early morning sun. The green and gray canyons were filled with shadows. Now, incredibly, they crossed in moments where the horseback journey had taken hours.

"Drop us down in the badlands, near that tallest spire," Mr. Halliday requested of the pilot, pointing toward the sandstone wonderland they were approaching. "The boys think they can begin in this region and follow their map."

A few minutes later, the helicopter hovered over the spot and then dropped straight down to land on a level area. Halliday got down and helped Karen from the plane, and then the two boys scrambled forward and through the bubblelike cockpit.

The pilot, a pleasant young redhead, got their sleeping bags and food supplies and dropped them onto the ground beside them.

"If I have time, I'll fly up early tomorrow and circle around till I spot you. Otherwise, I'll meet you about four o'clock at this same spot to take you back to the ranch. Is that the plan?"

"That's right," Mr. Halliday was now standing beside his three young friends. "If these kids haven't found what they're looking for by then," he added with a smile, "they'll have to give up the search till next year."

"Good luck!"

The pilot waved to them and closed the bubble. With a puttering roar and a great swirl of air currents, the amazing contraption gave a jerk and rose toward the sky, but Dan had already turned away. He was gazing eagerly at the fantastic scene around him. This must be like the landscape of a dead planet, he thought with awe.

There was no vegetation nearby—only a vast area of

(131

eroded, buff-colored cliffs and rocks rearing grotesquely against the horizon. But the eerie scene did not dismay him.

"Bring out your map, Robert." Dan took from his own pocket Dr. Binns' translation of the scrolls found in Daniel Glover's cane.

"The first thing we have to do is compare this key with the landmarks drawn on your map. We should have no trouble in identifying that 'needle' this time."

15
The Phantom Pony

"I know we must be in the right area now."

Dan, seated on his pack, looked from Dr. Binns' translation to the map. "See that mark?"

"Gamma," put in Robert, who was looking over his shoulder.

"Well, it corresponds to this mark on the map, above Signal Point. Now, here it says, 'Ride due east across seven canyons.' I know we've crossed seven canyons because I counted them from the plane when we flew this way from the Point. Then it says . . . Say, what's this?"

He stared in amazement at the key to the map. They had been so busy getting ready for the impromptu trip that they had had no time to study carefully the instructions laid down by Daniel Glover for his brother.

"This is goofy, Rob. Under this triangle symbol—*delta*,

(133

isn't it?—are these words: 'You will see the Old Lady of Threadneedle Street.' What is that supposed to mean?"

The other boy began to laugh. "It's a good thing I read an illustrated book about London once," he remarked. "The Old Lady of Threadneedle Street is the Bank of England. It's the name of a building shaped like a flatiron. Old Daniel was just dragging a red herring across the trail. He thought only another Englishman would interpret that correctly."

By this time, Karen was perched on a small rise of land, looking all around. Suddenly she declared, "There it is! There's a big cliff, shaped just like an iron." She pointed to a wedge-shaped hill off to the northeast.

Robert went to stand beside her. "Karen's right," he agreed. "It looks like the building in London."

The cliff was not far away, and soon the four prospectors had shouldered their packs and were on their way, passing many weird formations as they went. Within an hour, they had reached their objective and had climbed up and were standing on the end of the "flatiron."

"What next?" asked Mr. Halliday. He was letting the three eager adventurers run the show, but he was as keenly interested as they were.

"Well, from here," Dan said, after consulting his papers again, "we are supposed to get a glimpse of that camel we missed before."

He looked out hopefully at the strange formations in the wasteland before them. There were thousands of odd shapes in the eroded land. There were castles and towers and nuns with bowed heads. He found Lincoln's profile and a buffalo head, but he could find absolutely nothing among the formations that reminded him of a camel.

Mr. Halliday had taken out his binoculars, and Robert and Karen were turning from side to side, as they, too, scanned the rocks. A dozen times Karen shouted a false alarm and pointed to some tortured formation which she wishfully took to be the camel, only to be scoffed at by her more realistic cousin and brother.

They were beginning to get anxious, when the Bar-Alpha foreman began to chuckle. "You'd better start lifting your sights," he suggested. "I'm afraid you can't see the forest for the trees. The rocks have you all confused."

Puzzled, Dan lifted his eyes and looked far off toward the horizon. At the same moment Robert cried, "There it is! It isn't a rock formation at all!" He pointed off beyond the valley, where another range of mountains rose purple against the sky. "There it is, in those mountains—a perfect camel with two humps!"

"I see it, too." Karen jumped up and down, and Mr. Halliday hastily caught her arm and pulled her back from the edge of the cliff.

Dan himself was the last to spy the formation and then he laughed at his own blindness. Once spotted, "the camel" was so obvious that a baby couldn't miss it.

"Now, from this flatiron rock, where we now are," he told his excited listeners importantly, "we are supposed to walk directly toward that camel, keeping it always in sight. 'Walk until the head of the camel disappears,' Great-grandfather tells us."

"That looks like a pretty substantial mountain to me," Robert remarked wryly. "How could it just disappear?"

"Well, let's climb down and follow instructions," suggested Gordon Halliday, "and see what happens. I just hope the gold mine isn't way off there," he added. "We'd have to call off our search for sure."

From then on the fantastic quest became more difficult. The party traveled for hours through the rugged area, carrying their heavy packs. The sun rose high in the sky, with no cloud to soften its glare. It was breathlessly hot, even in the shade of the rocks, when they stopped for lunch.

When they started on again, the camel still lay before them, far away on the horizon—unchanging.

Then, surprisingly, a portion of the mountain to their left seemed to shift as they walked toward it, and got in the way. The head of the camel vanished behind it.

"The head has disappeared!" Dan exclaimed. He stopped to wipe his dripping forehead on his sleeve. In spite of the heat, his excitement was mounting. "There's just one more landmark to spot, before we can go to the Phantom Pony."

"I remember what that is!" Robert declared. He had no need to look at the map. "It's a formation called Punch and Judy." They had wandered down again into the rocky wonderland, and now they stopped once more to look around.

Karen's small face was a picture of dismay. "Why, there seem to be dozens of pairs of rocks that could be called Punch and Judy," she said.

Dan had been studying his papers again, and he laughed now, exultantly. "But only one right pair," he said. He pointed to two huge, eroded rocks, standing face to face, like a pair of dumpy puppets. The biggest one had an "arm" raised toward its mate.

" 'Punch gives Judy a punch in the eye,' " he quoted from

the key to the map. "Now we are instructed to look between those two characters," he said in a tense voice. "We are supposed to see the gray walls of another canyon. When we reach that canyon, we should find the Phantom Pony Mine."

Karen let out a little squeal. Then she and Robert were racing toward the knoll on which "Punch and Judy" stood.

Robert reached it first and climbed up on it, standing precariously on the sloping sandstone as he peered between the two figures.

"What do you see?" Karen called from below.

"Nothing." He looked discouraged when he came sliding back down the knoll to join his companions. "There isn't a sign of any gray canyon through there," he said flatly. "Just more rocks like this, and above that, oceans of trees.

"Are you sure you read those instructions correctly, Dan?" he asked.

"That's what Dr. Binns' translation said," insisted Dan. "I hope he didn't make an error in his Greek."

He sat suddenly down on a ledge of stone and slipped off his heavy pack. It would be heartbreaking if their trail had reached a dead end after all their efforts, he thought. They were already exhausted, and the rendezvous point, where they were to meet the pilot of the helicopter, was miles behind them.

Meanwhile, Mr. Halliday had climbed up on the rock to check Robert's observations. When he came back, the boys and Karen were in a huddle, poring hopelessly over the now tattered map.

Then Dan began to laugh. His voice squeaked a little

in sheer relief. "How dumb can we be!" he exclaimed. "No wonder you couldn't see that cliff, Rob. You were looking through from the wrong side."

"See?" He pointed to the map. "The trail to the mine circles around this way and goes back toward the northwest. You have to take your observation from behind Punch and Judy."

Dan climbed up behind Punch and Judy to demonstrate. From that perspective, the opening between the rock puppets narrowed to a few inches. Centered in that opening, like the detail in the viewfinder of a fine camera, was the gray stone face of a distant canyon wall. It lay far up the mountain.

With renewed enthusiasm, Karen and the boys readjusted their packs and turned their faces toward the heights, walking single file behind Mr. Halliday. Again, their leader made careful calculations with his compass, for their last objective kept appearing and disappearing from sight.

It was a rough trek. Long before it ended, Karen, who had started the day so angelically, was having difficulties and worrying everyone. First, she had the bad judgment to sit down to adjust her pack in the very middle of a bed of black Arizona ants.

Before she knew it, the huge insects had spread over her clothes and up her bare arms. She squealed with anguish as they began to bite, and the party had to halt for a full fifteen minutes while she got rid of the pests and doctored herself with insect lotion.

They had scarcely started off again when she disobeyed Mr. Halliday's instructions not to stray from the group, and darted impulsively out of line, to look at a pretty yellow flower in a ravine, brushing past the only cactus they had seen that day. She came back with her right shoulder looking like a pincushion.

"It *jumped* at me," she insisted. She sat on a rock while Mr. Halliday carefully extracted the poisonous barbs, one by one, from her quivering flesh. Her lips were trembling but she stubbornly refused to cry.

"It didn't jump at you!" her brother retorted. "You ran right into it because you were goofing off."

Dan was frantic not only because Karen's escapades were delaying their progress, but because he knew how much those poisonous little barbs burned and stung.

Even Robert, usually more patient, was getting restless. He looked anxiously toward the sun, which was falling westward.

"It's late," he remarked, "and we've still got a rough climb ahead. I hope we reach the canyon in time to do some scouting today. I'm just beginning to realize," he added wryly, "why that yellow stuff they call gold is so precious."

Halliday laughed as he put his tweezers back into the first aid kit. "Nature makes it hard for man to find, all right," he said. "If she didn't, I guess it wouldn't be worth going after."

Still wincing, Karen drew her blouse back over her shoulder and buttoned it again. She was now a weary and bedraggled little girl, and by the time the day's journey was over, Robert had taken her knapsack and Dan had added her bedroll to his own.

It was almost sundown and they were all nearing exhaustion when they finally came out of the woods and arrived at a deep canyon. Standing at the edge of it, they found themselves face to face with the bare granite wall they had seen from afar. A small stream gleamed faintly below.

Tired as he was, Dan was all for starting right off to locate the mine. "It can't be far from here," he declared. "According to the map, it's across this canyon. The last entry on Daniel Glover's scroll shows the mine below the forelegs of the Phantom Pony."

"Just what do you think he meant by that?" Robert was frowning. "I don't see anything that looks like a horse."

"Well, it could be a rock formation," suggested Mr. Halliday, "Or it could be one of those Indian paintings we've seen along the way. You sometimes find pictures of animals scratched on the walls of canyons.

"But whatever it is," he added firmly, "I want you all to sit down and rest for a few minutes. Then you boys can take off into the canyon for a look while Karen and I set up camp. We've done enough hiking for today."

"That looks like a good spot to camp," said Robert, pointing to a grotesque pile of sheltering rocks along the rim of the canyon.

Dan agreed with his choice, and the two boys carried their own gear and Karen's to a niche in the rocks. Then they sat down and tried to relax. Karen, who was still in bad grace with the boys, asked for her knapsack and produced four juicy oranges, which she passed around.

But Dan and Robert were too keyed up to waste time. They had scarcely devoured their fruit when they were on their feet again and away to the canyon's edge, eager to climb down, cross the stream, and make their first exploration.

The canyon was already in shadow, so they worked

against the gathering dark, but they checked out every jutting rock they saw that even faintly resembled a pony. They looked in vain for petroglyphs, Indian rock paintings, which might have given them a clue to the whereabouts of the lost mine. They looked along the canyon for signs of old diggings.

But they found nothing.

Not until the canyon was in darkness did they answer Gordon Halliday's yell from the rim of the canyon, and admit defeat.

Weary and disillusioned, they climbed back up to join him and Karen around a glowing campfire. They ate the steaming stew their companions had prepared, but were too disappointed to care what they put into their mouths.

After supper, Dan got the map out once more, trying to figure out where they had gone wrong. Had he missed a clue, in spite of all his care?

"There's this picture of the setting sun," he remarked, pointing to a rayed half circle near the final landmark. "Does that ring a bell with you, Robert? Or Karen?"

"I saw that," said Karen, "but I think it just means the end of the trail."

Robert shook his head in disgust. "That's what I figured. But it could be some last, crafty joke of the Glover twins. Don't forget, they had a secret language, Dan, and a secret code. That setting sun might be a sign they used that nobody else will ever understand."

"The mountain could have changed, too, in seventy-three years," Mr. Halliday suggested. "Perhaps there was a horse carved by nature across the canyon at one time, and it's no longer there."

142)

"Well, we didn't have much time to search tonight," Dan admitted, with an accusing glance at Karen. "And we won't have too much time tomorrow, if we have to get back to meet the plane by four o'clock."

It was a trio of anxious young prospectors who hit the sack that night, high on Mystery Mountain. Dan Glover's throat ached as he lay wide-eyed, looking up into the star-spangled sky.

He imagined that he saw a winged pony fly through the constellations and disappear in space. Could they come so close, he wondered, and still fail to find the mine?

16

Eureka!

Dan Glover fell into sleep as he watched the imaginary pony vanish into the ether. He awoke battling a windmill. The arms of the windmill seemed to be waving somewhere above him, making a terrible racket.

Dan opened his eyes, to discover Karen leaning over him. She was banging with a stick on a tin can, her face full of mischief.

"Wake up, sleepyhead!" she cried.

Still in a daze, Dan sat up in his sleeping bag, arms flailing, and struck his hand on the edge of the can.

"Ouch!" he screeched. "Get away from here, you little pest. Haven't you caused enough trouble already—falling off of rocks, wasting time for everybody? You're nothing but a jinx. I must have been soft in the head to let you come along in the first place. We'll never find the Phantom Pony if you——"

"I'm sorry." Karen moved out of his way. "But it's late, and if you don't get out of there, you won't have a chance to look for the mine. Robert is already up, and breakfast is ready."

She moved off with a fling of her dark curls.

Dan knew she was right. The early sun was slanting through the trees. He crawled out of the sack and put on his shoes. Then, still disgruntled, he got his jacket from a tree limb and joined the others at the campfire.

The aroma of sizzling sausage hung in the cool air.

"You have only two or three hours, boys, to make a final search of the canyon," Mr. Halliday remarked as they ate. "We promised to meet our pilot back there in the badlands at four o'clock, and it's a long, hard trail."

Dan and Robert looked at each other ruefully. After their discouraging search of the previous evening, they weren't feeling quite as confident as they had at the beginning of their trip.

Robert put down his fork and went to get his map. He spread it out on the ground beside Dan. "I've looked at this thing till I could draw it with my eyes shut," he stated, "but I still can't figure out that pony business."

"Maybe it really is a phantom," said Karen, undiplomatically, "and never existed at all." She moved around to sit beside the boys, and they pointedly ignored her.

"We must be in the right spot," Robert was saying. He pointed to the map. "There is that prominent gray cliff that rises across the canyon. Here's the sign of the setting sun, which can only mean the end of the trail. . . . Now,

(145

the pony is pictured right on the face of that blank wall, and——"

"The mine should be under it, nearby," said Dan.

Karen was staring at the map. A puzzled look came gradually over her young face. She put her finger on each of the four sides of the map, her lips moving as she did so. "North, West, South—East," she said mystically. She ended by pointing at the rayed circle.

"Why do you insist on calling that the setting sun?" she asked, almost casually. "It's east of the canyon——"

"We've been over all that," Dan told her impatiently. "That's just a symbol that means——"

He stopped speaking, but his lips remained open as he stared unseeingly at Karen. Then he rose slowly to his feet, pivoting, to look at the sun.

His heart suddenly bolted within him. Why that was it—the final clue! Drawn plainly on the map was, not the setting sun, but the *rising* sun.

Before Karen and Robert could ask any questions, Dan was on his way. He tore past the campfire and ran to the base of the craggy pile of rocks at the edge of the canyon. In a few minutes, he had climbed to the top of them and was looking west across the canyon—to the face of the rocky wall.

It glowed pale and pink in the light of dawn, and there, before his eyes, was the Phantom Pony. Unmistakably clear, the figure seemed to be riding across the rock, and it was truly a phantom—a giant shadow painted by the morning sun as it shone from behind the pile of rocks upon which Dan stood.

Dan lifted his arms and waved them and saw the movement of his own shadow atop the dark figure.

His feeling of triumph was so tremendous that he couldn't contain it. Half-sliding, shouting as he came, he scrambled down the rocks to a spot where the others were eagerly waiting.

"Eureka!" Dan cried to the heavens. "Eureka! I've found the Phantom Pony!"

In a very few seconds, all four of them were standing at the canyon's edge, looking across at the amazing phenomenon.

"Well, I'll be hanged!" muttered Gordon Halliday. "It's the perfect image of a running horse. No wonder Daniel Glover called it the Phantom Pony."

"It's almost like a miracle," said Karen softly.

"It sure is," agreed Robert. "You'd have to be standing right in this spot, in the early morning, at the right season of the year, to see the shadow exactly like that."

"And if it hadn't been for Karen we might never have noticed it," Dan admitted. He looked appreciatively at his sister.

"I take back everything I said about you, Karen," he added with a grin. "Well—almost everything! You're still a pest, but you aren't a jinx. If we find the mine below that horse, we can thank you."

"Well, what are we waiting for?" Robert said then. "I see a little ravine over there. The mine must be right about there. Come on," he shouted. "Let's go!"

Dan flew to get the short-handled shovel Mr. Halliday had carried, and the miner's pick. Moments later, they were on their way down into the canyon. Dan thought he could almost smell the gold.

They had no trouble in finding the ravine. They had

(147

missed it the night before because it was slanted, and hidden by the contour of the rocky wall.

Dan leading, they climbed eagerly up the steep wash, fully expecting to see the opening of Daniel Glover's gold mine before them. But they stopped abruptly a third of the way along, dismayed to find their progress barred by a pile of rocky rubble.

17
The Golden Gleam

At first, the two boys were simply sunk at the sight of the dam of rock that lay before them. Then Robert climbed back down into the big canyon to take another look at the shadow of the pony. He returned looking determined and confident.

"That mine has to be here," he said flatly. "This spot is right under the forelegs of that ghost horse. There must have been a flood or landslide that covered the opening to the mine."

"What do we do now?" asked Dan.

"We dig," said Mr. Halliday, who had been standing quietly by. He bent over, picked up a big rock and threw it down the incline.

Soon they were all busy, passing rocks down and throwing them out of the way. When the bigger rocks were removed, the boys took turns with the shovel. Karen set about the job without protesting, even when the rough rocks scraped her hands.

It was grueling work. Though the canyon was pleasantly cool when they began, they were soon perspiring and panting. They kept at it for a good two hours without finding a single clue to the presence of a mine. Dan was almost ready to give up in despair.

He straightened up, resting his aching back against the side of the wash.

"What's the use?" he said in disgust. "I don't think Daniel Glover or any other human being has ever been around here. We haven't seen a single sign of——"

"Hold it!" Robert suddenly cried out. He was wielding the short shovel and it had struck something different. There was clang of iron against iron.

The boy went on working, furiously and silently, while the others waited. At last he reached down and pulled something into the light. It was part of a rusty old shovel, mute evidence of human labor.

Dan made no further protest, but set to work again with redoubled effort. Soon the head of a miner's pick was uncovered, and they could see that a rubble-strewn opening lay there, beneath the ledge of the hill.

The next big discovery was an outcroping of quartz that, in some prehistoric era, had bubbled from the earth like wax. Mr. Halliday bent down and struck off a piece of the rock with his pick.

Karen and the boys stopped their work and waited, scarcely breathing, as he examined it.

"This is it, kids," the man said at last. "There is absolutely no doubt about it. We have found Daniel Glover's

gold mine. This rock is gold quartz, just like those speci-
mens you found in the old chest back at the ranch. And if
this assays as rich as that does—and there is enough of it
—your fortunes are made."

Dan and Robert just stood there, looking at each other.
Now that the big moment had come, they found that they
couldn't even speak. After all their dreams and all their
searching they were actually standing on the site of the
fabulous mine, lost to man for seventy-three years.

"How about that, Rob?" he said finally. "Hundreds of
prospectors have been up on old Mystery looking for this
mine, but *we* found it, you and I—and Karen."

Robert's shining face at that moment exactly matched
Dan's own. "You and I and Karen *and* the Greeks," he
said exultantly. "Don't forget that old Plutarch and Archimedes had a hand in this discovery, too!"

Karen, playing her tiny pocket flashlight along the pro-
jecting vein of quartz, let out a squeal of delight. "Look
what I found. A big piece of gold!"

While Dan and Robert looked on, Mr. Halliday hacked
out a section of the rock with the pick. He showed it to
Dan. It emitted a pure yellow gleam.

"That's what you call free gold," the man remarked.
"The nugget you see there is almost pure. Looks as though
you've really found the mother lode," he added.

"Boy, if it's that easy to find," Karen said innocently,
"why don't we just buy a helicopter and bring it up here
and take back a whole load of gold?"

"It's not quite that simple, Karen," said Mr. Halliday
with a smile. "Finding a gold mine is just the first step to
riches. There won't be much free gold like that, and there
is really a lot of work involved in getting metal out of ore.
You don't just chip off bagfuls of the stuff."

Both boys looked serious at that. They, too, had been up in the fleecy clouds of a dream world. Now they came back to earth with a bump and began to think.

"Just what do we have to do to get the mine in operation, Mr. Halliday?" Robert asked.

"First, you will have to put up a monument of discovery," he replied. "Seems as if Daniel didn't even get around to doing that. It can be a four-foot post or a three-foot pile of rock near the entrance to the mine, containing a discovery notice properly signed. Then you have to file a mining claim at the recorder's office."

"That sounds simple enough," put in Dan.

"That's just the beginning. . . . After that, we'll hire a geologist to come up here and figure out the extent and direction of the lode. You'll need proper surveys and a half dozen more monuments to mark the points of your claim."

"This is beginning to sound complicated," said Robert, in some dismay. "Don't forget, Mr. Halliday, Mother expects me to start back to Boston in the morning."

"Don't worry about that, Rob," Dan told him. He was beginning to feel a new sense of responsibility, now that he was a partner in a potentially valuable enterprise. "Mr. Halliday and I can take care of the business affairs. In fact" —he looked straight into his cousin's brown eyes —"I think it's about time we made Karen and Mr. Halliday equal partners with us in the gold mine. After all, they both helped us find it."

"That's a great idea!" Robert was in perfect accord. "What do you say, sir?" He turned to the ranch foreman. "Will you continue to advise us for a quarter interest in the mine? We can all be equal partners."

Before replying, the tall Westerner took off his hat and

scratched his graying head. Then he held out his hand to the boys and Karen, each in turn.

"I'll accept that offer," he said. "Of course, I need a gold mine about as much as a horny-toad needs a ruffled petticoat. Miss Charlotte keeps me in luxury down at the Bar-Alpha. But you three partners will need help."

He looked from one to the other of the intent young faces. "For one thing, you will be required to do yearly work on your mine, to keep your claim valid. This is government land, you know. Chapo Robles and I can help you with that during your summer vacations. And sooner or later," he continued, "we'll have to decide whether to set up a mill and work the mine ourselves, or whether to lease the Phantom Pony to a big mining company."

"Well, we can decide those things later," Danny declared happily. He had never felt better in his life. "We might even work out a secret code, as the Glover twins did," he suggested to Robert. "Then we could write down our plans——"

"Just don't write to me in Greek," Robert interrupted him with a grin. "I can't read it."

"And I can't write it," Danny retorted. "But you know," he added thoughtfully, "it might not be a bad idea. I may decide to take Greek when I go to college——"

He stopped short, startled at his own words. It was the first time in his life that he had ever expressed any interest in a college career. He had to admit now that there was much to learn in this old world, and a fellow couldn't just spend his whole life riding a horse over the Arizona hills, pleasant though that might be.

He glanced up to meet Karen's teasing eyes.

"I never thought I'd hear Danny Glover admit that

(155

there is any good in stuffy old book-learning," she said. "You've changed a lot this summer, brother dear."

"In some ways I have," Dan admitted proudly. "I still want to be a rancher and run the Bar-Alpha, and I want to help operate the mine, too. But I intend to do it right, and I know I've got lots to learn."

"Well, that's in the future, Dan." Mr. Halliday interrupted the conversation. "Meanwhile, time's a-wastin'. If we're going to meet our pilot, we'd better shoulder our packs and get started. Hide those old, rusty tools, boys, and come along.

Dan and Robert hid the ancient pick and shovel under some rubble; and then, somewhat reluctantly, they left the mine and followed Karen and Halliday out of the ravine. But after they had climbed up from the canyon, the triumphant pair just couldn't keep from stopping at the rim to take one last look. They stood straight and tall as two identical saplings.

"I still can't quite believe it has happened, Dan," Robert remarked. "In the past two weeks, we've climbed mountains together—we've flown in a helicopter—we even solved an old murder mystery——"

"And best of all," put in Danny, "we rediscovered the Phantom Pony Mine, and it's ours."

Just then, dark-haired Karen came back to stand for a moment between them, looking outward across the canyon.

"See—the 'pony' has disappeared!" she exclaimed. For the sun had now risen high in the sky and the canyon was filling with golden light.

The Author

FLORENCE LAUGHLIN spent a happy childhood with her three brothers and one sister in the little prairie town of Crosby, North Dakota. She used to entertain her smaller brother and sister with wonderful tales out of her own imagination. When she was fourteen, the whole family moved to San Diego, California, by way of a motoring trip through Canada and the eastern states—camping, she says, in the middle of New York City! She left San Diego State College after two years, to be married. Mrs. Laughlin has two children and now lives in Tucson, Arizona, where she keeps house for her son and for their dog, Socrates, studies desert lore, and writes articles, short stories and books for children—mostly mysteries.